BRINGING BACK KAY–KAY

DEV KOTHARI

WALKER BOOKS

First edition 2024

Library of Congress Catalog Card Number pending
ISBN 978-1-5362-3364-3

23 24 25 26 27 28 XXX 10 9 8 7 6 5 4 3 2 1

Printed in City, Country

This book was typeset in TK.
The illustrations were done in TK.

Walker Books
a division of Candlewick Press
99 Dover Street
Somerville, Massachusetts 02144

www.walkerbooks.com

For Keya and Vira.
You know, right?
And for Abhi.

I

That morning, before I found out you were missing, Kay-Kay, I was home alone, feeling sorry for myself.

While you'd been at camp, things had been so different for me. Summertime finally started to feel a bit special. Ma cooked my favorite dishes for a change. Dad took me with him when he went shopping or to the club. And it was only a handful of times that either of them commented on what I did or how I did it—telling me I should do it properly, as you would have done. Toward the end of the two weeks, I felt like Ma and Dad were finally starting to see me. The way you see me. Of course, I'd missed you while you'd been away, but for the first time in a long, long time, life felt so light and easy. It was as if I'd been sitting in the shade for too long and I'd finally stepped into the sun.

Pathetic, right?

I'm sorry, Kay-Kay. I think that morning, when Ma and Dad were running frantically up and down the platform at the railway station looking for you, I was still in my pajamas sipping chai, wishing you'd be away for a little while longer.

Careful what you wish for. Isn't that what Nani always said? I wish, I so wish, that I'd been more careful. Because without you, there's no sun, no warmth, no light.

There never will be.

When Dad called to ask if you'd come home yet, I said something like, "Aren't you supposed to be picking him up?"

"Just answer the question, Lena," he yelled. Then he swore. Dad, our dad, swore. Actually swore. I couldn't believe my ears.

"No," I whispered, fear creeping into my thoughts. *Where are you? What's happened?*

"Call me immediately if he shows up," Dad said in a choked voice.

"Y-Yes, but what's going o—?"

He hung up without another word. I thought of calling him back, but I knew he'd get more angry. I kept opening the front door, staring out at the stairs leading up to our apartment to check if you were coming. When the doorbell rang, I ran so fast to open it that I slipped and fell, banging my knee on the coffee table. But it was only the newspaper boy. I slammed the door in his face, poor guy, and threw the rolled-up *Deccan News* across the living room. Then I quickly scrambled to get it like a dog chasing a stick in the park. God knows what I was expecting to find in it—news of a train accident, a natural disaster—no idea. After pacing up and down the living room about a hundred times and chewing my fingertips raw, it finally occurred to me to call Samir. Of course! He'd have come back on the same train as you.

I remembered seeing his phone number on a Post-it stuck on the desk in your room. The first time I called him, he didn't pick up, but I kept calling. He finally answered after the fifth time.

"Hello, Samir?" I said.

I heard muffled sounds on the other end of the line—the phone being passed around.

"Samir, are you there? It's Lena."

"Hello, Lena beta. This is Mrs. Pratap talking."

Samir's mum! God, she is the worst of all the aunties. I always marvel at how you can be so nice and polite to her. I can't even bear the way she talks—sickly sweet and so fake.

"Auntie, is everything OK? Has something happened?"

She tutted. "Oh, no, beta! You don't know? You poor, poor child."

"Is my brother not with Samir?"

"I don't know if it's my place to tell you. What if your parents take offense?"

Yes, she actually said that. It took everything I had to not scream into the phone.

"Please, Auntie," I somehow managed to say. "I'm really worried."

"I don't know what to tell you. It's such a terrible tragedy. But Karthik did not come back with Samir."

This time, I was not calm. "What do you mean? What happened?"

"What to tell you, Lena? Karthik did get on the train with Samir yesterday evening, but then he disappeared. No one can find him. It's so . . ."

I don't know what she said after that. I didn't hear her anymore. I didn't hear anything, except the pounding of my heart. A moment later, Kay-Kay, when it all sank in, I collapsed onto the floor in a crying heap.

What had happened to you?

SCHOOLBOY GOES MISSING FROM TRAIN

Fifteen-year-old Karthik Krishnan, who was returning home to Lamora after attending a summer camp in Goa, has gone missing under mysterious circumstances.

Mrs. Rita Varghese, lead coordinator at Wildlife Adventures, said Karthik had attended a two-week camp along with three other students from Saint Vincent's School in Lamora. A camp coordinator accompanied the four boys to Margao Junction on Saturday, May 13, where they boarded the ERS–Lamora Overnight Express at 5:15 p.m. When the train arrived at Lamora Junction at 6:43 a.m., 53 minutes later than its scheduled arrival time, Karthik was nowhere to be found.

Samir Pratap, another member of the group, said the four boys had dinner together at 9:30 p.m. and had gone to their berths soon after. Mr. and Mrs. Krishnan, who were waiting to pick up their son at Lamora Junction, enlisted the railway police's help as soon as it became apparent that Karthik was no longer in the party. Other than his backpack, a thorough search of the train resulted in no clues.

Karthik's distraught parents are desperate for any news of him. Mrs. Krishnan broke down in tears while speaking to the *Deccan News*. She said, "Karthik means everything to us. We love him so much. We just want him back."

Several people in the local community have expressed their shock and concern over Karthik's disappearance. The *Deccan News* spoke to Mr. D'Angelo, principal of Saint Vincent's School, which is still recovering from a recent incident in which a fire injured three students and one teacher. Mr. D'Angelo said that parents and teachers are struggling after yet another blow and are praying for Karthik's safe return. He described Karthik as a top-ranking and talented student who recently took the Class 10 board exams.

The devastated family has filed a First Information Report (FIR) at the Lamora Central Police Station. Inspector Rana said the police are pursuing all avenues of investigation and urgently appeal to anyone with any information to come forward.

2

Once the newspaper article came out, the phone wouldn't stop ringing. We'd all rush to pick it up, but it was Dad who usually got there first, with a worried "Hello? K-Karthik?" Ma and I would look on anxiously. But within a moment or two, we'd realize it was only another so-sorry-to-hear-about-your-son call. Ma would go back to sitting on the sofa, alternately staring into space and crying, and I'd sit back down next to her on the edge, biting my nails and wondering again and again where on earth you could be.

Waiting felt like torture, so I busied myself doing things for Ma and Dad. Dad would nod his head when I made cup after cup of chai. Ma would give me a half smile when I'd cook Maggi noodles or khichadi and hand her a bowl. But she'd just push her food around. And Dad seemed to survive on tea alone. After Dad had been to the police station or Ma had spoken to one of the aunties, they'd shake their heads and tell me "No news yet." They knew I was there, and yet it was like I didn't exist.

But I didn't really care about that anymore.

I'd look at them and see only lines—dark lines that appeared out of nowhere on Dad's face, wiggly lines of tears on Ma's face, crisscross lines of their interlaced fingers. Most times, once I'd made sure there was nothing more I could get for them, I'd just go to my room and cry into my pillow.

It was hard enough without you, Kay-Kay. I couldn't watch their pain too.

3

With each day, the mood in the apartment got worse and worse. Ma started looking the way she did a couple of years ago, after Nani died, spending more and more time locked away in her bedroom. And when she was with us, she was there but not there. Dad sat silently next to the phone, sipping cup after cup of tea. It was as if hope was deserting them.

So many times, I wanted to take them by the shoulders and shake them.

Do something! Anything! I wanted to yell.

I swear, one time I almost threw my favorite mug (you know, the cheesy one you got me, the *Best Sis in the World* one?) at the wall, simply to break the awful silence. I think that was the moment I finally realized I had to do something more than making chai and cooking food and doing chores.

I'm sorry, Kay-Kay. I wish I hadn't waited so long.

4

The next time I saw Dad getting ready to go to the police station, I was in the hallway before him, with my shoes on.

"What're you doing?" he asked, the question creasing his forehead.

"I'm going with you." I opened the front door and stepped out.

He opened his mouth, probably to say *No, you're not*, but instead he glanced toward his and Ma's bedroom, where Ma had caged herself. Then he nodded and closed the door behind us.

The mid-morning sun blazed in the sky, and traffic blared on the road. As Dad navigated the car carefully around the buses and auto-rickshaws and scooters, I stared out the window, wondering how the world could go on as if nothing at all had happened.

At the police station, a round-faced constable with gray hair and a gray mustache asked us to wait in the corridor. Dad sat down on one of the benches lining the grubby green walls. I walked up and down, reading the notice boards, trying to see if I could gather any news. They were littered with faded posters of missing children and wanted men and yellow notices of government rules.

"Inspector Rana, one minute, please," Dad said, standing up as a policeman walked up the corridor from the other end. I raced to his side.

"Mr. Krishnan. You're here again." Inspector Rana sighed. He was a big man, with a wide face framed by thick eyebrows and a thick beard. His snug khaki uniform was starched and neat but discolored by sweat patches.

"Is there any news?" Dad asked.

"Sir, please," Inspector Rana said. "As I told you yesterday and the day before, if there is any news, we will call you."

"But it's been five days!" The words came out of my mouth before I realized I'd opened it. "You must've found something."

Inspector Rana cocked his head and said sharply, "Who's this?"

"Sorry, Inspector—this is Lena, my daughter," Dad said quickly. "Karthik's younger sister."

The inspector raised an eyebrow. "Mr. Krishnan, go home. We'll get in touch with you when we have some news." He put a hand on Dad's shoulder. "Coming here every day is not going to solve anything, is it, now?"

Dad's shoulders sagged as he nodded slowly.

Anger bubbled up inside me. Why is he giving up so easily?

"What are we supposed to do? Sit at home and do nothing?" My words came out stronger and louder than I'd intended.

"Lena!" Dad snapped at me, but Inspector Rana patted his shoulder as if to say *It's OK. I'll handle this.*

The inspector narrowed his eyes at me. "Yes. You *should* stay at home and let us do our jobs. For all we know, your brother will be back in a day or two."

"What do you mean? Why do you think he'll be back in a day or two?" My mouth went dry. "Wait . . . Is there . . . something . . . you're not telling us?"

Inspector Rana let out a loud, impatient sigh and beckoned the round-faced constable standing a few paces away.

"Patil," he said to the constable, "how many children go missing in our country every day?"

Constable Patil shuffled his feet. "Hundreds, maybe even thousands," he said.

"And what is the number one reason for their disappearance?" Inspector Rana barked.

Constable Patil looked at me kindly and said in a quiet voice, "Most of them are runaways, sir."

"Karthik didn't run away. He would never run away." A flush of heat rushed up my neck and face. I pulled at Dad's arm. "Dad, tell them, please."

"Lena is right, sir," he said. "There's no reason for Karthik to do something like that."

Inspector Rana let out a soft grunt, then looked directly at Dad. "She *may* be right. But can you say with absolute one hundred percent certainty that your son didn't run away? He's a teenager, almost a grown man. How well do you know him? Do you know absolutely everything that's going on in his life? Can you say confidently there's no reason, *not one*, for him to think of leaving home?"

Dad blinked and opened his mouth, but no words came out.

"Just go home, please," Inspector Rana said in a condescending tone.

Annoyed, I said, "There is no reason. Not even one. Karthik did not run away."

But the inspector remained expressionless as if he hadn't even heard me.

"You just don't care!" I couldn't help getting angry at his disinterested behavior. "You just don't want to do anything. You can't even be bothered to talk to us nicely. What kind of a policeman—?"

"Enough! Do not raise your voice at me." The inspector glowered.

Dad gently pulled me back and said, "Sorry, sir. She's just worried about her—"

"Why are *you* saying sorry, Dad?" I glared at the inspector. "He's the one who should be apologizing for not doing anything to find Kay-Kay."

Constable Patil looked at me pityingly as his boss's face flickered with anger.

"Mr. Krishnan!" the inspector said without taking his eyes off me. "Go home and wait, like I told you. Let us do our jobs."

I felt Dad's hands on my shoulders.

"Sorry, sir," Dad said again. "Please excuse us." As he dragged me down the corridor, I turned around and glared at Inspector Rana, who had not moved. When he caught me looking, he yelled, "Mr. Krishnan, I better not see your daughter at my police station again."

That was the moment I knew I had to look for you myself.

I was going to find you, Kay-Kay, if it was the last thing I did.

5

Ma opened the door before Dad could even turn the key in the lock.

"What did the police say?" she asked, clutching him by the arm the moment he stepped inside.

I closed the front door softly behind us and looked at Ma. Her hair was disheveled, her eyes swollen and small. She hadn't showered for days. She was still wearing the same pink sari, stained with the chai I'd forced her to drink in the mornings, sip by painful sip.

Dad gently removed her hand from his arm but kept on holding it. "Let's sit down."

Ma refused to move. "Is there any news? Any news at all?"

"No, Nalini . . . there's no news yet," Dad whispered.

Ma shook like a leaf in the wind, and I grabbed her shoulders to steady her.

"Where is my Karthik?" she howled.

"Ma, the police—" I began.

"The police will find him soon, Nalini. Don't worry." Dad shot me a look and stole the words from my mouth. How thoughtless did he think I was?

"Come, dear. Let's get you freshened up." Dad steered Ma toward their bedroom.

I stared at my feet as they left me standing in the hallway.

Outside, the sun blazed hot and strong. Hardly any rickshaws raced past, and even the motorbikes seemed to have lost their roar. The quiet outside mirrored the quiet inside. Dad had gone to work. Ma was asleep in her bedroom. Alone in the living room, the creaky ceiling fan whirring warm air around me, I reached out for the home phone.

As I dialed your number, once again I wondered how much easier it would've been if I had a phone of my own. I couldn't really blame anyone else for that, though. Had I let you help me with my studies, my grades would've improved long ago, and Dad would've already bought me a phone, like he promised. As it was, I'd turned down your offers, imagining the look on Dad's face when I showed him my next report card sparkling with top grades that I'd got without *anyone's* help. But of course, that hadn't happened. You know full well how I can't even sit and study and concentrate for an hour, let alone hours on end, days on end, the way all the top students like you do. And now, when all my friends already had their own cell phones, all I could do was sneak around like a thief, trying to use the home phone to begin my investigations.

"The number you are calling is currently switched off. Please try again later," I mouthed the words along with the nasal voice of the woman from the recorded message.

"You bet I will," I said, cutting the call.

I dialed Samir's number next. I never really liked talking to him, never liked him at all, actually. I never understood how the two of you could be best friends. It was like a gentle dove being friends with a flashy peacock! But ever since you told me how you first became friends, when he stood up for you against the gunda-mawali boys at the soccer field who were messing with you for no reason, I tried to be civil no matter how annoying or haughty I found him.

I had to call a few times before he picked up.

"Hello, Samir?" I said.

"Yeah." He sounded sleepy.

"This is Lena. Karthik's sister."

After a long pause he said, "Yes?"

"I . . . I just . . ." Now that I had his attention, I didn't know quite what to ask.

"Yes?"

"Did Karthik say anything to you?" I blurted out.

"What do you mean?" he asked.

"I mean you were with him at camp. Did something happen? Did he say anything? You must know—"

"I don't know anything," Samir said firmly. "Nothing happened."

"But—"

"Look, the police questioned me and Raheem and Zubin. We told them everything we knew. There wasn't much to tell. We got on the train, we had dinner, we set up the sleeping berths in our compartment, then we all went to bed. And in the morning, he was gone."

My fingers gripped the phone tighter as if trying to squeeze out something more from Samir's words.

"Are you still there?" he said. "Listen, I've gotta go, OK?"

"Wait! Please! Could you think a bit more? Maybe you'll remember something." I knew I was clutching at straws. "Samir, Karthik is your best friend. Don't you care? Don't you want to find him?"

"Best friend, huh?" Samir said, his voice suddenly low before he went quiet altogether. After several moments,

I heard some shuffling in the background, then he said, "Listen. I don't know where Karthik is. I don't know what happened."

"But—"

"I *really* don't know anything. I've got to go n—"

"Are you guys not friends anymore? What happened?"

"Gotta go," he said loudly, then hung up.

I sat there for a while, holding the phone, a strange feeling taking hold in my stomach like a stirring or a fluttering. Like when you're in a car going uphill on a winding road and you're not really sick but you aren't quite right, either. I tell you everything, Kay-Kay. What happens at school, what new disappointment I add to Ma and Dad's list, what Ayesha and I get up to after school, even silly things like what we do in our two-person Great Girl Explorers Club. Everything! And I didn't even know that you and Samir had fallen out.

I took a deep breath.

I was going to find out. Find out everything about you.

Because that was the only way I would find you.

I gently pushed open the door to Ma and Dad's bedroom. A waft of cool air greeted me from within. The curtains were drawn, and the fan was at full speed. Ma was sleeping on her side, facing away from me. I stepped inside and scanned the room, looking for your backpack—the one that was found on the train. Nothing on the near side of the room. I tiptoed around the bed, hoping Dad hadn't put it in the closet with the creaky door.

Do you remember one time when I was little, maybe six or seven, and I'd become convinced that closets were where monsters lived? Especially ones with creaky doors? You brought me here to show me it isn't true. You carefully took out all of Ma's saris and then you took my hand and made me go in to see. Hours later, Ma and Dad had found us sitting inside, giggling and laughing and singing funny monster songs we'd made up. You always know how to make me feel better, Kay-Kay.

I looked at Ma's sleeping face. She seemed so peaceful, with her arm hanging over the side of the bed. The maroon curtain fluttered in the window, and a beam of light flashed on the floor under Ma's outstretched arm. I saw the navy strap of your backpack poking out from under the bed. Of course, Ma wouldn't have let it leave her sight. I dragged it out quietly and tiptoed from the bedroom.

As I studied your navy-and-orange backpack, in the too-bright afternoon light of the living room, I suddenly saw you standing in front of me. You were wearing a plain white T-shirt; your favorite blue jeans, torn up at the knees;

and those raggedy red sneakers. You picked up that back-pack and slung it on one shoulder.

Bye, El-Kay, you said, pushing back the black hair falling on your forehead. *See you when I get back. Try not to get in trouble while I'm away. And please try not to empty the nankhatai jar, will you?* You waved at me, grinning that dimpled grin that makes your whole face light up.

Can't promise that! I stuck out my tongue at you. *Bye, Kay-Kay. Oh, and please will you try not to be the best at everything at camp?* I said as you disappeared through our front door.

I took a deep breath and forced myself to look through your backpack, now sitting, lonely, on the sofa. There were only clothes in the main compartment—jeans, shorts, T-shirts, pajamas, a towel. I took them out, shook them in the air, turned their pockets inside out, all while trying not to inhale the pine-forest deodorant scent on them. Your scent. In the top pocket, I found your toiletry pouch and a book called *The Prophet*. In one side pocket, undershirts and underpants and in the other, some socks. Nothing at all out of the ordinary.

Standing up, I held the empty backpack upside down and gave it a good shake, but nothing fell out. I put it flat on the floor and tapped it with my palms from top to bottom.

My hand felt a bulge near its base. Odd. When I looked inside, I found another zipped compartment. Inside was a small square package wrapped in rainbow-striped paper. Written in one corner were two little words:

For El-Kay.

My heart skipped a beat.

I unwrapped the paper carefully and found a round metal case and a small rolled-up strip of paper. Unfolding it with trembling hands, I read the short message you'd written on it:

Because no adventurer can be without one . . .

A sob rose in my throat. I gritted my teeth and pushed it back down.

Inside the round metal case was a compass. I held the cool, smooth metal in my hands, thinking how you'd held it too, barely a week ago.

Remember that time we were all watching *Around the World in Eighty Days?* How I kept wowing at all the places Phileas Fogg goes to? Dad kept asking me to sit still and calm down. But, of course I didn't. I barely heard him, I was so excited and at one point I exclaimed, "I am going to

do that! When I grow up, I will go around the world too!"
And that's when Dad said, "Traveling the world is not an
ambition. It's a hobby for people with no ambition. There's
no need to fill your head with these ridiculous notions,
Lena. All you need to do is learn from your brother and
study harder. God knows your grades need improvement."
I finally went still then, trying not to feel crushed, and you
grimaced at Dad's back. The next day when I came home
from school, you handed me a book about Amrita Sher-
Gil. And the following week, it was one about Mary Kom.
And then Anandibai Joshi. For weeks afterward, you kept
bringing me books about Indian women pioneers until
the crushing feeling disappeared.

Flicking the compass open, I watched the little red-headed
arrow swing from side to side before pointing north.
    I blinked.
    It was pointing to your room.

6

I heard the annoying beeping the car makes when it reverses. Dad was parking, just back from work. The harsh afternoon had already turned into a mellow evening. Quickly, I returned everything to your backpack except the compass, the wrapping paper, and the book and carried it to Ma's bedroom. Luckily, she was still asleep. I put it back where I found it and crept out again.

I was just heading into my bedroom when I heard the front door open.

"Lena," Dad called.

I hurried to cram the book, the compass, and the crumpled wrapping paper in my desk drawer. It would barely close.

"Lena!"

"Coming," I yelled, finally slamming the drawer shut, praying I didn't break anything. I rushed out of my room hoping Dad wouldn't notice my flushed face.

"How's Ma been?" He sat down on the sofa in the living room, taking his shoes off. He didn't notice my face. He barely looked at it.

"She's been sleeping since you left," I said, trying to keep my voice even.

Dad sighed heavily.

"Shall I make some chai?" I asked.

He nodded and went to wake Ma. I headed to the kitchen, willing myself to be patient. It would only be a matter of half hour or so, until our silent tea drinking ritual finished, until I could escape to my room and have a proper look at your things.

As it happens, it took a lot longer than I thought.

A heavy, stifling silence surrounded us as we sipped hot chai. I looked at Ma's swollen eyes and the lines on Dad's face and felt a pang in my chest. I opened my mouth, but what could I possibly say that would make them feel better? Luckily, Ayesha called and rescued me.

"Hey, Lena." It was so good to hear her sweet voice even if it was far away, nestled in the beautiful hills of Shimla.

"Hey, Ayu," I said.

"Is there any . . . ?"

"No."

"Sorry, Lena. How . . . ? How are . . . you?"

I knew she'd be biting her lip and twirling-untwirling strands of her long hair with her fingers. She always does that when she doesn't know what to say. You know what she's like, right? Worrying about saying the wrong thing, worrying about her words hurting others. Not a bit like me, who always blurts out the first thing that comes to my head.

But right then, all I could do was whisper, "I am fine . . ." even though what I wanted to say was that I was terrified for you. So terrified I could hardly sleep at night. So angry I wanted to break and smash and shatter things. So upset that I felt hollow and useless, like a dried well.

"I know you're not fine." Ayesha sniffled. "But they'll find Karthik and everything will be OK."

"Uh-huh," I said. I wasn't going to cry. If I did, it would only make things worse for Ma. She was still sitting on the sofa, staring into space. Dad had gone into the kitchen to put the cups away.

"It will be OK, Lena," Ayesha promised. "I know it will. I heard Ammi talking to Raheem's mom the other day. Everyone is worried and praying for Karthik . . ."

"Yes."

"I'm sorry I can't be there for you. Ammi said there are no train bookings available. She sends her love. And Fatima too."

"Tell them I said hello," I said, trying to make my voice sound as normal as I could.

"I will. I know I can't do much from here, but call me if you need anything OK?"

My best friend's words wrapped me in a soft, warm hug. As we were about to end the call, a thought flickered in my head.

"Hey, Ayu . . . do you think your ammi might have Raheem's number?"

"She might. Why? Do you want to talk to him yourself?"

"I was thinking it couldn't hurt, right? I mean I already spoke to Samir. But he wasn't much help. You know what he's like. But maybe . . . maybe . . . Raheem might remember something."

"Yes, makes sense . . . You never know. Hold on—let me go ask Ammi."

Ayesha returned a few moments later with Raheem's number, which I hastily jotted down on a piece of paper. I thanked her and we said our goodbyes. As soon as I was back in my room, I went to my desk to look at the things

I'd stuffed in it earlier. That's when the doorbell rang.

It was the Mehras, from 5C. Of course, then I had to make chai again and get the biscuits and namkeen out and sit on the sofa, nodding politely as the Mehras tutted and said things like "What can you do when something like this happens?" and "What really is in our hands, anyway?" Every time I felt the urge to snap at them, I looked at Dad's tired face and forced myself to keep my lips sealed. Besides, responding to them would only make them stay longer. After they finally left, it was dinnertime and I had to help Dad in the kitchen. So it wasn't until bedtime that I finally got to the drawer again. I emptied it and put all my own things in an old shoebox, which I slid under my bed.

In the empty drawer, I carefully placed the compass. After smoothing the crumpled rainbow paper and unrolling the strip of paper with your message written on it, I put them in my science textbook. Then I picked up your book. It looked old; the back cover was ripped slightly, and the pages fanned out from the spine. On its plain algae-green cover was printed in simple lettering

THE PROPHET BY KAHLIL GIBRAN.

I opened the book, and tucked between the first pages, I found your train ticket.

It even had the ticket collector's check mark.

It's OK. It's OK.

I put the ticket in the drawer. Then I thumbed through the book. It was a book of poems. I never knew you liked poetry, Kay-Kay. They had titles like "On Love," "On Pain," "On Children." I tried reading some. But I could barely concentrate on the words. When I turned the page to a poem called "On Friendship," I found a piece of lined yellow paper folded in half, slipped between the book's pages, covered in your neat handwriting.

A Friend

Inside jokes. Silly banter.
Someone to laugh with.
Listening ears. Shoulders to cry on.
Someone to rely on. cry with. count on

Roller coasters. Sandcastles.
Someone to eat ice cream with.
Hideouts. Tree houses.
Someone to share secrets with.

> Maps with X's. Hidden clues.
> Someone to treasure-hunt with.
> Lighthouses. Constellations.
> Someone to find the way home with.
>
> Buddy.
> Ally.
> Pal.
>
> You.

A teardrop splatted on the page, smudging some of the words in the poem.

Your words.

Your poem.

I gently wiped the smudge and read your poem again. And again and again as questions whirled up a storm in my head.

Where were you?

What had happened to you?

And who was the "you" in your poem?

7

We are on a beach. Just the two of us.

An orange sun is setting over a stretch of glittering blue. You are wearing a white T-shirt and blue jeans and your trademark red sneakers. You run away from me. "Catch me if you can!" You grin. Annoyed, I chase you, slipping in the silken sand. My arm stretches out to catch you. But you are always just out of my reach. Then a white light blinds me. A fireball sun blazes red over our heads. We are climbing a mountain. I am still chasing. You are still out of reach. Suddenly everything goes dark. I am in a tunnel. Running. Running. Running with my heart pounding, my legs throbbing, chasing your silhouette in the distance as the tunnel twists this way and that.

"Kay-Kay!" I yell.

My voice echoes in the dark tunnel.

"Kay-Kay!" I yell again.

But you still don't answer.

"Shhh . . ." I heard a voice.

"Where are you?" I gasped.

"Wake up," said the voice. I felt a hand gently shaking my shoulder. When I opened my eyes, I saw Dad sitting by my bedside. I blinked. My heart was still racing.

"It was just a dream," he said.

I sat up, wiping my clammy hands on the bedspread. As Dad looked at me with concerned eyes, my heart returned to its normal rhythm.

"Lena, I . . ." He didn't finish. Instead, he took my hand in his and fell silent. He was dressed for work but his clothes were wrinkled, his hair hastily brushed, his glasses smudged.

"Dad?" I said, suddenly panicking about what this could mean. "Is it . . . Kay-Kay . . . ? Have you heard anything?"

He quickly shook his head. Then he took off his glasses, rubbed his eyes, and said, "I know how hard things are . . . And I can see how much you're doing . . . helping around the house and with Ma—"

"It's nothing really, and I don't mind helping at all."

I looked at Dad's tired face, wishing I had something better to say to him.

He put his glasses back on. "I don't know . . . I just . . ."

"It's all right, Dad. I am sure Kay-Kay's fine. And he will be back soon. I know he will be . . ." My voice tapered off, getting lost in the darkness of doubt.

Dad's shoulders slumped and he looked away. A few moments later, he patted my hand, then got up and headed to the door. "I have meetings all day today," he said, turning back to face me. "I've made breakfast and will get some dinner on the way home. Ma's resting. Can you sort out lunch?"

I nodded, feeling glad to be able to help Dad somehow. At least, with it being summer, I could be at home with Ma so he would worry a little less.

"Good. Call me if any—"

"Yes, I will," I said quickly, not wanting to hear his voice crack.

Then he left.

And I was alone again.

The first thing on my list that day was to call Raheem.

As I listened to the phone ringing at the other end, I stared at the wall where all your awards and medals and certificates are hung up. Remember how I used to tease you by calling it the Kay-Kay Glory Wall? You always smiled awkwardly when I said that or when Dad bragged about you, pointing out the wall to anyone visiting. "Isn't he clever, my son?" Dad would insist on the guests taking a closer look at your awards and certificates. "When I left my village to come to Lamora for a better life, all I could do was settle for an ordinary office job," he would tell them. "But not my Karthik. He will become an engineer or a doctor. He will make my dreams come true." Dad would beam as you stood uncomfortably next to him.

Staring at the wall then, I realized how embarrassing it must've been for you. I felt bad about teasing you, and when someone finally picked up the phone, I was glad to have my train of thought interrupted.

"Hello?" I said. "May I speak to Raheem, please?"

"Speaking," said a boy's deep voice at the other end.

"Hi, I'm Lena."

"Hey, hang on a sec?"

I heard muffled voices in the background followed by the sound a door slamming.

"Hey, sorry about that. That was my little pest of a brother. He's such a nuisance. Super annoying. Like, all the time. Lena, is it?"

"Yes, I'm Karthik's sis—"

"Oh."

I cleared my throat and answered the question before he could ask, "There's no news yet."

"Oh. I'm really sorry, man. What happened was totally messed up. Like, he was with us when we got on the train and had dinner and then he just *poof!* Umm . . . Anyway . . . umm . . . sorry. How can I help you?" Raheem sounded uncomfortable.

"I'm trying to figure things out, you know. I was wondering how things were before he . . ." I couldn't say the words.

"Sure, sure. I understand. What d'you wanna know?"

"Can you tell me what happened on the train?"

"Sure. Like, we got on the train fine at Margao. A little later after we settled in our compartment, Zubin suggested we play cards to pass time till dinner. Karthik and I were game, but Samir was acting a bit weird. I mean, even weirder than he usually is. Anyway, he agreed eventually and then when he realized that we'd be playing mendicot, he said he didn't want to partner with Karthik, which was a bit awkward . . . you know . . . but it wasn't a big deal, we just put him with Zubin and me with Karthik . . . So anyway, we played a few games of mendicot, and it was actually pretty fun. Karthik and I had a couple of very good wins . . . Later on, we had our food and joked around a bit at the sink, where it was a big squash, all trying to brush our teeth at the same time. Then afterward, we set up the sleeping berths and bunked in for the night."

"So that was the last time you saw Karthik . . ."

"Mmm . . . yes . . . yes . . . I think so. I mean I vaguely remember seeing someone getting up in the middle of night . . . probably to go to the bathroom . . ."

"Was it Karthik?" I asked quickly.

"I don't know. Maybe? But to be honest, it was so dark, it was hard to tell. It could've been Karthik or Samir or Zubin . . . or I might've been dreaming, you know?"

"I understand."

"When I woke up in the morning, Karthik's berth was empty and I thought he'd probably gone to the bathroom. But as the train got closer to Lamora and he still wasn't back, we started looking for him. We called his phone, but it was switched off. We looked up and down the train carriage, even in the neighboring ones, but we still couldn't find him . . . It was so weird. We couldn't work out what on earth could have happened to him. Then at Lamora Station, we hung around to help your parents look for him on the train till the railway police arrived . . ."

A few moments passed in silence as the dust of disappointment settled all around me.

"Er . . . Lena? Are you still there?"

"Yes . . . yes. I'm still here—sorry," I said.

"It's OK. No problem. Was there anything else you wanted to know?"

"Yes, actually. Can you tell me a bit about the camp?"

"About the camp? What do you mean?"

"I mean . . . did anything out of the ordinary happen at camp with Karthik? Did he say anything? Did you see or hear anything?"

"No . . . Not really. It was just camp stuff, you know. We were busy all day long doing water sports or hiking or rock climbing or whatever. And Karthik was never in my group for any of the activities. Plus, I shared a room with Zubin. So I don't really know what to tell you . . ."

"I just thought—"

"I know. I'd do the same if I were you. But to be honest, I don't really know him that well. He's more Samir's friend. Which, actually, I've always thought was strange—I mean, *interesting*—they're so different . . . you know. Sorry, what am I even talking—?" "Yes, I know," I mumbled, sifting through what I had learned from the conversation.

Raheem doesn't know anything. And he can't be the "you" from your poem.

"Anyway, sorry, there's nothing much else I can tell you."

"Will you call me if you remember anything?" I said, even though I knew he probably wouldn't.

"Yeah, of course. No problem. If something pops into my head, I'll give you a call right away," Raheem said.

"Also, can you please give me Zubin's number?"

"Zubin? I don't know if he'll tell you anything different."

"But still?"

"Sure . . . yeah . . . OK. Hang on a sec—lemme find it for you."

Raheem gave me the number before we hung up. I called Zubin, but he didn't pick up.

Then I tried calling your number again and got the same recorded message.

Dead end again.

I wanted to scream and shout at the top of my lungs, but I knew Ma was asleep in the next room. Instead, I picked up a sofa cushion and threw it across the living room; it narrowly missed the blue lamp in the corner. I was sick of dead ends. I paced up and down for a while. Simply sitting at home staring at dead ends wasn't an option.

I needed a plan.

And for that, I needed to be like you. Organized.

I got a piece of paper and a pen and started writing in my neatest handwriting.

WHAT MIGHT HAVE HAPPENED?

1. Some sort of accident
2. Someone did something to you.
3. You ran away.

THINGS I'VE FOUND OUT

1. Nothing was found on the train other than your backpack.
2. Your phone is missing.
3. You and Samir are no longer best friends.
4. You like poetry and you like to write poetry.

THINGS I CAN DO

1. Talk to Zubin
2. Talk to Samir again to find out why you fell out
3. Search your room
4. Talk to someone at the camp (That woman from the newspaper article?)

Inspector Rana thought that you'd run away. He even got Dad thinking it. But if you did, surely you would've taken your backpack with you. And you wouldn't have bought a present for me. Besides, you would never leave us. You simply wouldn't. No! I crossed that out as an option.

Somehow, writing it all down made me feel better. It helped me make sense of the thoughts swarming in my head like bees. I finally understood how your detailed, color-coded study plans must help you.

Do you remember that time, last Diwali, when you were working on a new study plan for the rest of the school year? You took it to school every day, to work on during recess. And one day it had disappeared from your backpack. You couldn't find it anywhere, and you had to start all over again. You didn't get mad, like I would've. In fact, Ma was more upset about it than you were. "Oh, Karthik, you put in so much effort. It must've taken you hours."

I'm sorry, Kay-Kay. I was the reason it disappeared.

That day Dad had been yelling at me.

"How can you let your room get so messy? It's worse than a pigsty."

"Look at your desk. Even the raddi-wala keeps his scrap tidier than you!"

"Learn *something* at least from your brother, for heaven's sake. How you two could be siblings and be so different is beyond me!"

It was the same. Always the same. But that day, while you were out, he led me up to your room to show me how perfect it was. He lectured me about the "importance of organizational and planning skills" like you had, about "appreciating the value of things" and about how "time once gone, never comes back."

Something snapped in me that day—I don't know why. When I saw your backpack under your desk, with your perfect, neatly scribed study plan peeking out, it was too much. After Dad left the room, I just took it. Then I went back into my room, slammed the door shut, and I ripped it to shreds.

I really am sorry, Kay-Kay.

My plan to look for you looked nothing like your study plan. It was more like a bunch of lists, really. But I hoped it was a good plan. Perhaps one that even *you* would be proud of.

8

I logged on to the home laptop and found out the phone number for the camp coordinator, Mrs. Rita Varghese. Not only did she speak with me when I called her, but she also answered all my questions patiently while I took notes.

Q: Did you meet Karthik?

A: Yes. I met all sixteen kids at the camp, your brother included. I saw each of them at some point every day depending on the day's schedule.

Q: Did the camp go as you expected? Did anything unusual happen?

A: No. The camp ran as scheduled. This year there were no accidents or even minor injuries. The troop leaders reported to me each evening, when we would review how the day had gone, including things like accidents and injuries, participant ability and performance, participant spirit and morale, food and nutrition, etc. All in all, this camp was as routine as they get.

Q: What kind of activities were included?

A: Adventure and sports activities like walking and hiking, river rafting, rappelling, beach volleyball, and cricket. Educational activities like expert talks and group discussions. Whole-group activities such as bonfire night, a treasure hunt, and board game night.

Q: How did Karthik find the activities?

A: From what I saw and the reports I got from the troop leaders, Karthik was one of the most engaged members of the entire camp. He participated in everything and seemed like a very talented and intelligent boy. A natural athlete. One of the troop leaders did mention to me that he was a bit on the quiet side, perhaps not as loud and boisterous as the other boys. But in my book, that is not a bad thing!

Q: Is there anything else you can tell me?

A: Not really. As I told the police and the newspaper, on the final day of camp one of the troop leaders dropped Karthik and his friends off at the station. He waited until the train left to make sure they were safely on board.

Q: Is there nothing else at all?

A: I'm really sorry, but there isn't.

Q: One last question. Can you tell me anything about the others from Karthik's school who were on the camp? Samir, Raheem, Zubin?

A: (A long pause) I'm not really sure I should . . .

Q: Please, Mrs. Varghese. Was there anything about the other boys that was unusual or out of the ordinary?

A: (A short pause) Hold for one moment. (Noises of a chair screeching, paper shuffling.) OK, I see here from our reports that one of the boys in the group requested to switch rooms.

Q: Who was it?

A: I suppose there's no harm in telling you. It was Karthik's roommate, Samir.

Samir. Samir. Samir! Remember that time a few years ago when he came up to me in the playground one afternoon and told me that you'd been in an accident? He looked so worried when he said, "What are you still doing here? Run. Go tell your parents." And I did. I ran home as if my clothes were on fire and told Ma and Dad, and they rushed over to the hospital immediately. And when you turned up just after they left, completely fine, I was so relieved and confused and afraid of what Dad might say, I started crying. You calmed me down and made me drink some chai. You spoke to Ma and Dad so I wouldn't have to. You were gracious when Samir called later to apologize. But you know what I never told you, Kay-Kay? For weeks after that incident, every time I came across Samir, he laughed at me and said "It was just a joke. A joke!"

Samir lied then and he was lying now. Something happened between you at camp. I had to find out what. So I called him again. He answered but didn't even let me ask anything. "Look Lena. Like I told you before I do not know anything. So please stop calling, OK?" Then the line went dead.

I gritted my teeth. I was just going to have to talk to him in person. Somewhere in public, where he wouldn't be able to weasel out so easily.

9

"**W**hat're you doing?" Ma's voice startled me. I was sitting on the sofa in the living room, scribbling on my lists. When she came in, I was smiling because I'd figured out the perfect place to speak to Samir.

"Nothing . . ." I quickly folded the paper and put it in my pocket as Ma came and sat next to me. She'd changed into a fresh sari. The flowery scent of Ponds talc wafted around her. I stole a glance at her face to see what kind of mood she was in and was relieved to see that she looked calmer. I followed her gaze as she stared out of the big double windows with the afternoon light filtering in through them.

Outside, a lone bird chirped cheerfully and a tiny smile appeared on Ma's lips. I found myself smiling too as my heart hurtled through happy memories. I saw her in the kitchen making kheer, tasting it again and again to get it just right. Or in the vegetable market, scolding the vendor about the state of his tomatoes. Or in my room, shaking her head at the dirty socks on the floor, saying, "Not again, Lena." I missed that. Even her disappointments in me. I missed her.

Ma looked at me and took my hand. *Maybe she is feeling better.* I squeezed her hand and leaned into her. I waited, hoping she would wrap her arms around me, hug me tight, let me cry into her neck.

But the hug didn't come.

Instead, she remained still, with a vacant expression on her face.. On the outside she looked OK, but I knew that her illness was getting worse. I knew this wasn't just worry for you—it was more than that. The last time she was like this was when Nani passed away. Remember? Throughout the thirteen days of mourning, Ma barely ate or drank or slept. She just stared into space. You never left her side. You watched over her, bringing her water and food, singing the songs that Nani used to sing to her, till the dark clouds hovering over her thinned. Funnily enough, I can't remember what I was doing then. Not that anything I would have done would have helped. It always seemed to me that while you could instantly make her feel better, I had the knack for doing the exact opposite. Even now, instead of thinking of Ma and what I could do comfort her, I was thinking about how I wanted to be comforted.

Ma sighed. "It's so quiet without Karthik," she whispered. "I see him everywhere. Every place reminds me of him. Everything reminds me of him. Day or night. He is all I can think of."

That's exactly how I feel too. But look, Ma, look at my lists. Don't worry: I'm going to find him.

I opened my mouth, but instead of words, only a puff of air escaped my lips.

Ma's face wasn't dry anymore. "I'm sorry, Lena," she said. "I've been so . . . Everything was going so well. But now . . . I don't know. I don't know anything anymore. I'm . . ."

Ma began to sob. I sat down on the floor in front of her.

"It's all right," I said, bringing her hands together in her lap. I held them tightly as her shoulders shook. "We will find Karthik. Everything will be OK. You will be OK. And we'll go back to how things were."

She kept on crying. I wiped the tears from her face with her sari pallu.

"Why don't we watch some TV till Dad gets back?" I jumped up and looked for the remote. "How about one of those old black-and-white films you like?"

I switched on the TV, flicking through the channels.

"Look, Ma." I wiped her tears again. "I think it's the one with the three funny brothers. What's it called?"

She looked up.

"Why don't I make us some chai and we can watch the film together," I said.

She nodded and I hurried to the kitchen, eager to do something, anything that would help Ma feel better. But as I made the tea, my mind wandered down the same dark thought alleys it knew so well. The shadows in those alleys always seemed to whisper the same things. Lena is not good enough, not smart enough. Lena is not the one Ma and Dad want, not the one they love.

My hands shook as I strained the tea into two cups, splattering some of it onto the kitchen counter. I wiped the splatters away and quickly brought my mind out of the shadows. Now wasn't the time. Ma was waiting. When I went back to the living room with the tea and some biscuits (Marie for Ma and Parle-G for me), a melodic voice singing a wistful song drifted from the TV.

Ma had fallen asleep where she sat. I set the tray down

and propped a cushion under her head. I turned the volume down but left the TV on.

At least, I thought, *she isn't hiding away in her bedroom.*

I gently pushed your bedroom door open and felt a knot in my stomach as I looked inside.

The room was exactly as you'd left it. The neatly made bed with the blue-and-white-striped bedspread. The desk with a stack of red notebooks and a bouquet of sharpened yellow pencils. The pinewood wardrobe and the brimming bookcase in the corner by the window. There were no posters on the wall, not like in my room. Only your study plan above the desk. No dirty socks on the floor. No mess.

The knot in my stomach tightened, and my feet rooted themselves in the doorway. And then I got this image of you. Sitting hunched over your desk, buried in books, your hair falling on your face. You turned and gave me a mischievous grin, almost as if you were saying, *What're you waiting for?*

Steadying myself, I stepped inside.

I began with your desk, leafing through the notebooks, shaking them in the air. Nothing out of the ordinary. Desk drawer next. Nothing. I opened your wardrobe and looked through your shirts and T-shirts swaying on the hangers, through the neat piles of folded clothes. Nothing. I shuffled the books in your bookcase, then looked through each and every one of them. Nothing. I looked behind the book-case, stood on your bed and looked above the wardrobe. Nothing. I looked under the bed and dragged your sports bag out. I took out the tennis racket, cricket bat, the table tennis paddle, and all the balls that go with them. Nothing. I even shook the blue window curtains.

There was nothing I could find in your room that would help me.

Not. One. Thing.

Leaning back on a wall, I slid down to the floor and sat there, my head resting on my knees, surrounded by your sports equipment. I had been so sure I would find some-thing. Something that would give me a clue about what happened between you and Samir.

Or maybe something about the "you" from your poem. Perhaps you had a crush on someone. *No, that couldn't be,* I thought. I knew how focused you were in your studies. You studied and studied and studied like twenty hours a day. When would you even have had the time to think about things like that? Perhaps the "you" was a new friend. Someone you met recently.

I was caught in the maze of my thoughts. I needed a way out. But I hadn't found anything in your room that would help.

My cheeks started getting warm as anger simmered inside me. I wanted to yell at you for being such a goody two-shoes. I wanted to rip your notebooks, throw your clothes, and scribble all over the walls. Instead, I forced myself to calm down by listing my top ten favorite films.

Remember the first time you made me do that? We were at Auntie Priya's house, playing Monopoly with our cousins. And Mona cheated. She plain stole money from the bank, so I yelled at her and she started crying. When I asked her to stop being such a baby, she got all tomato-face, and called *me* a liar. Then she pulled my hair and I completely lost it. I don't even remember how Auntie Priya's ugly vase got in my hand. Before I could do anything stupid, you pried my fingers off the vase and pulled me onto the balcony.

I thought you were going to yell at me, but instead you grinned your dimpled grin and said coolly, "Hey El-Kay, I think we should watch a film later. We'll pick one you like. Tell me, what are your top ten favorites?" I still remember standing there staring at you, completely baffled by the question. But of course, somewhere in my brain a little thought was already running through a list of films trying to work out which ones to include in my top ten, and by the time I'd finished, the injustice was almost forgotten.

I would never mess up your room.

One by one, I put all the items back in the sports bag, then zipped it up and pushed it back under the bed. But it got stuck halfway through. I pushed it harder, but it wouldn't budge. I moved it sideways and with one tiny little push in it went. Surprised, I stuck my head under the bed and that's when I saw it. A little black bag hanging from one of the bed slats. I reached underneath the bed and yanked it down.

There was nothing special about the bag. It was as ordinary as canvas bags can get.

But inside it, I found the most extraordinary of things.

I found your poems.

All of them.

10

Ma was still asleep on the sofa when I slipped on my shoes and headed out of the apartment. I raced down the stairs, clutching the black bag.

I almost crashed into old Mr. Lobo from 1A on the first-floor landing.

"Watch where you're going, young lady!" he yelled.

"Sorry, Mr. Lobo," I called, swerving around him.

As I ran across the ground floor lobby toward the building gates, I heard Dad calling me from the parking lot. I screeched to a halt and turned around.

"Where are you going? Is everything OK?" he said, coming to meet me. He had his briefcase in one hand and a Saravana Bhavan takeout bag in the other.

I hid the black bag behind my back. "Yes. Everything's fine," I said.

"Where's Ma?"

"She's upstairs, sleeping." My feet itched toward the gates.

"Where're you going?"

"Out," I mumbled, and turned to go.

"Stop!" Dad said sharply.

I stopped.

"Out where, Lena?"

"To Ayesha's."

Dad arched his eyebrows. "I thought they were in Shimla."

"They came back. Ayesha called to tell me." Lies rolled off my lips like butter on a hot chapati.

He nodded slowly. "Be back soon."

"Yes, I will." I was already racing against the warm wind through the gates.

I ran down the street, not quite knowing where to go. It was early evening, and the traffic was light, with a few bicycles and scooters on the road and hardly any cars or rickshaws. I needed to find a place where I could sit undisturbed to read your poems. Someplace safe. I kept running, turning left and right avoiding people, stalls, dogs, vehicles. Where could I go? The playground would be crammed full, and I had no money with me, so a café was not an option.

A rickshaw honked loudly, veering sharply around me. A stray dog yelped, jumping to its feet, startled by the honk. As the rickshaw sped away, I realized that my feet had brought me to the perfect place. After taking off my shoes, I stepped across the threshold into the temple and rang the brass bell hanging from the ceiling. The marble floor led me on a zigzagging path, around people sitting cross-legged, toward the sanctum. With each step I took, I felt calmer and calmer. The air was filled with sweet jasmine incense and the pujari's prayer chants. In the sanctum sat the red-and-gold idol of Lord Ganesh, surrounded by lamps, incense sticks, and offerings of flowers and fruits and sweets. I put my hands together, closed my eyes, and bowed my head to him.

You must know what I prayed for.

The pujari handed me some prasad dana, crunchy little sugar balls. A blessing from Lord Ganesh, the one who removes all obstacles in our way. I needed it. I needed every blessing I could get.

Then I headed out through the back door of the temple to the rose garden and found an empty bench by the pond. Finally, I opened the black canvas bag. As I held the wad of your handwritten poems in my hand, I wondered why you'd kept them hidden away. And why you'd never told us you even wrote poetry!

Was it right for me to read your poems without your knowledge? But what if there was a clue in here that would help me find you? I clutched your poems tighter and tighter as I battled with these thoughts. Then I remembered how you once told me that although our hearts are smaller than our brains, they carry more weight in the decisions that we make. So I decided to listen to my heart and ask for your forgiveness later.

That's where I read your poems for the first time, in the peachy plum light of the evening sun surrounded by rose bushes. I found no secret, no clue in your poems. But somehow that didn't matter at that very moment.

Because Kay-Kay, your beautiful poems sucked the air from my lungs.

I could finally see you, as I'd never seen you before. For the first time, I saw your worries and your fears and your disappointments. I realized that I never really knew how you actually felt. And what is worse, I realized, I had never even tried to know. Not really. I was too busy feeling sorry for myself and complaining to you about my life.

By the time I finished reading, I could hardly breathe.

Then the clang of cymbals sounded from the temple as people started singing the aarti, the last prayer of the day. This helped me surface, and I gulped a lungful of rose-scented air. I put your poems back in the bag and headed inside the temple to join in.

It was dark when I got home.

I wished Dad trusted me enough to have a key to the apartment. I wished I could sneak in quietly instead of having to ring the doorbell.

Dad opened the door the moment I pressed it.

"Is that her?" Ma called from inside the apartment.

"Yes, Nalini." Dad ushered me inside, whispering as he did so, "Go and apologize to your mother."

"Why?" I said.

"Really, Lena?" Dad's brows furrowed. "Is this what you meant when you said you'd be home soon? Ma's been watching the clock for over an hour. Now go!"

I apologized to Ma, feeling a tightness in my chest. There I'd gone and done it again—made things worse. I spent the rest of the evening squirming on the sofa, trying not to disappoint them again.

That night, I read your poems over and over. I don't know how late it was when I finally put them in my desk drawer, next to the compass that had led me to them, and turned out my light.

I needed to sleep. But every time I closed my eyes, more questions popped into my head. Not just the ones I had lived with all week: What happened to you? Where were you? Why was your phone switched off? But also, Why did you and Samir fall out? Why were you writing such sad poems? What happened at camp? Did something happen even before you went to camp? And who was the "you" in that first poem?

Eventually, I gave up on sleep and got up. A sliver of light shone across the corridor under my bedroom door. I tiptoed toward the kitchen to get a glass of water but then found myself going straight past it and into the living room. Almost as if something were pulling me there. It was eerily quiet. The kind of quiet brought by the small hours of night. A streetlamp's hazy light cast distorted shadows on the walls—a cactus's prickly branches, a rakshasa's scary face, a vampire's fangs.

Shuddering, I picked up the phone and out of habit, dialed your number. I expected to hear the recorded message again, but instead I heard it ring.

My heart lurched.

Please, please, pick up. I gripped the phone as if my life depended on it.

Click! You picked up the phone.

"Hello, Kay-Kay?" I pressed the phone to my ear,

worrying I wouldn't hear you over the thump-thump-thump of my heart.

"Oh, crap!" a voice said.

"Hello?"

Click! The line went dead.

Desperately, I dialed again. And again. And again. But every time, I heard the annoying ding-ding-ding, followed by the recorded message.

I put the phone down and looked around the dimly lit room, scanning the scary shadows.

Is my mind playing tricks on me?

Am I imagining the voice in the same way as I imagined strange creatures in the shadows?

A shiver ran up my spine.

No. I had not imagined the voice. Not just that, but I'd actually recognized whose it was.

And it wasn't yours.

I walked up to the soccer field at the sports club, looking for Samir. The mid-morning sun blistered in the sky
as boys dressed in yellow-and-black uniforms ran up and
down the field. I scanned it, squinting, trying to spot
Samir's tall, fair figure. *He better be here.* I'd jumped through
a lot of hoops to get there. I had made chai and breakfast
and prepped for lunch, even though it was a Saturday and
Dad didn't have to go to work. I had apologized to Ma and
Dad again. And lied again.

My eyes smarted in the brash sunlight as I finally spotted Samir at the far-side goal, gesturing wildly at another boy, screaming something I couldn't hear. Coach Sir

beeped his whistle at them yelling, "C'mon, C'mon. Pass the ball!" Relieved, I headed toward the empty soccer shelter, which was littered with soccer bags, smelly sneakers, towels, and water bottles. I sat on a bench in the shade and waited for the practice session to end.

Not a single cloud floated in the sky and no breeze idled by. Even in the shade, the heat was stifling. I wiped the sweat off my brow and glanced at my watch. It had only been twenty minutes. I started rehearsing what I'd say to Samir.

"*Aarrrghhhhh!*" screamed a short boy with caramel-colored hair, sinking onto the field, clutching his ankle. Coach Sir jogged to him, shouting, "Carry on, boys, carry on," to the others. He inspected the boy's ankle and then hauled him up and led him over to the shelter.

Coach Sir's sweaty forehead creased when he saw me. "Who're you? What're you doing here?" he barked as he gestured for the boy to sit.

"Hello, sir. I'm Lena," I said standing up.

"Lena who?" He dug through a bag until he found what he wanted, then turned back to the boy and sprayed something on his ankle.

"Ufffff!" The boy winced.

"Chin up, young man!" Coach Sir said sharply, and the boy's face flushed red.

"I'm Karthik's sister," I said loudly.

Your name startled them both, and pity colored their faces. Coach Sir shook his head, and the boy stared at his feet.

"There's still no news," I said before they could ask. "I'm here to talk to Samir. I hope that's OK."

"Yes, no problem, beta. The practice is almost finished," Coach Sir said, his words dripping in sympathy. "I was so shocked when I heard. I don't know why such things happen to the best ones. Karthik was such a talented boy. I'd only heard good things about him from the other teachers. He could've gone far, very far . . ."

"And he will!" I said, gritting my teeth.

"Of course, of course, beta. I didn't mean anything by it." Coach Sir looked away, wiping his forehead. Uneasiness stretched around us as no one spoke. Finally, Coach Sir beeped his whistle and ran into the field yelling, "Time, boys. Start cooling down."

As I slid back onto the bench, I thought about how easy it is to hurt someone with a single careless remark.

I remembered this one time when Ayesha came to our apartment for a sleepover. We were watching a film and I can't remember exactly what happened, but I said something not-nice to her. (I won't repeat it. It's bad enough that I said it that time.) When she excused herself to go the bathroom, you switched off the TV. After saying nothing for several moments, you told me about this science experiment you'd read about. Three plants were placed in three different rooms. In one room, kind words were spoken, in the second, harsh words, and in the third, no words were spoken. Then you looked at me and said, "Tell me, El-Kay, which plant do you think grew the most?" I can still feel the heat of shame on my cheeks. When Ayesha came back, I hugged her so hard, we stumbled and fell. And as we laughed, rolling on the floor, you grinned your dimpled grin.

"Hey. You OK?" It was the boy with the hurt ankle, sitting across from me.

I nodded.

"Water?" He tilted his sports bottle at me.

"Thanks," I said, taking the bottle. I gulped down a few mouthfuls.

The boy took the bottle back and stuffed it in his bag. Then looking at me, he said, "I'm so sorry about Karthik. When we ate our dinner thalis together on the train that night, I never thought that that would be the last time I'd see him, you know?"

"You're Zubin?" I sprang to my feet.

He nodded, surprised by my exclamation.

"I called you yesterday."

"Oh, you did? Sorry, I must've missed the call," he said. "Why? I mean, was there something you wanted to talk about?"

"Yes. Yes, please," I said quickly. "I wanted to—"

"Lena! What are you doing here?" Samir strode into the shelter, his hair slick with gel. "She isn't bothering you, is she, Zubin?"

Before Zubin could answer, I said, "We were only talking." I stepped toward Samir. "I actually came here to speak to you."

"How many times do I have to repeat myself?" He paused. "I. Do. Not. Know. Anything."

Zubin stared at his feet as a few more boys arrived from the field.

"Yes, you do." I glared at Samir. "Tell me what happened between you and Karthik. Why did you switch rooms?"

A flicker of surprise showed on Samir's face. But a moment later, it was gone. "What's that got to do with anything?" he scoffed.

I wanted to tear his gelled hair out. Instead, through gritted teeth, I said, "Why can't you tell me what happened? What are you hiding?"

"There's nothing to hide." His eyes flashed with anger.

67

"I switched rooms because I wanted a room to myself. It had nothing to do with Karthik. Satisfied?"

"Not really," I said, trying to keep my own anger at bay. "Because you are lying through your teeth."

All went quiet as every eye in the shelter turned to Samir. Everyone knew something was about to happen.

Samir's face hardened. "Did you just call me a liar?" He stepped toward me.

I looked up at his face and said loudly. "Yes, I did."

He huffed, then cocked his head and said, "You want to know the truth? I switched rooms because Karthik, your brother, wouldn't stop bothering me with his nonstop grumbling and whining and that smug look on his fa—"

Before I knew it, I had charged into him and he'd staggered back in shock. I kept shoving as he retreated, and then fell down, tripping over a bag.

"You slimy weasel," I screamed in his face. "You horrible liar."

"Get off! Now!" he shouted, his face twisting with fear.

"Tell me what you did. Why do you have Karthik's phone?" I yelled. Now I could feel someone pulling me back. "What did you do to him?"

"Shut up!" Samir leaped to his feet again.

"I heard your voice last night. I know you have Karthik's phone. I know you did something. I'll tell the pol—"

"Shut your mouth!" he exclaimed, cutting me off. "Stop with your nonsense."

"Lena, leave it. Come on—this won't help anything." Zubin dragged me away from the shelter. I could hear Samir swearing behind me. "She's gone crazy. I mean, I know her brother is missing and all but did you see what she did? Ouch . . . ah . . . my back . . ."

I didn't turn around. I didn't look. I didn't need to.

You know, Kay-Kay, I will never ever forget the look of terror that swept over his face when I mentioned your phone. It was there for only a moment, but sometimes a moment is all you need.

Zubin and I walked away from the shelter and began to cross the field. Still fuming, I flumped down on the ground and pulled out a tuft of grass.

"It must be hard, huh?" Zubin sat down next to me.

I exhaled loudly, flinging the clump of grass and soil in the direction of the shelter, which was slowly emptying as Coach Sir ushered the boys to pack up and head home.

"Can I ask you something?" Zubin said.

"Sure." I squinted as the sun glared in my face.

"Why do you think Samir has Karthik's phone?"

"Umm . . . actually . . ." I picked up another tuft of grass as I debated whether I should tell him the truth.

"You don't have to tell me if you don't want to. It's

OK," Zubin said. "But you need to be careful. If it's true, it's quite a . . . quite a serious thing, you know. If there's a reason you think Samir actually has Karthik's phone, then the best thing to do would be to tell your parents, OK?"

He was right. You would've said the same thing, Kay-Kay. Come to think of it, Zubin seemed a lot like you. Calm and thoughtful. Not a bit a like me. I knew I shouldn't have gotten angry and picked a fight with Samir. But honestly, it was hard to keep my cool when I knew he was hiding something.

"You know, Lena," Zubin continued, "personally I think Samir can be a bit much sometimes. He's always up to something at school—cracking jokes in class, playing pranks during break, doing ridiculous dares and whatnot. And he does have a knack for taking things a bit *too* far. I mean, some of his pranks . . ."

I thought back to the day when Samir "joked" about you being in the hospital.

"But it's just who he is." Zubin shrugged. "Everyone at school knows it's best not to mind him too much."

"How can I not mind?" I said, anger spiking my words. "I only wanted to speak to him, but you saw what he did, right? I mean, as Karthik's friend, shouldn't he be *helping* me instead of behaving the way he did?"

Zubin sighed.

"Some friend he is!" I flung the tuft of grass high into the air and watched its dismal flight before it crash-landed just inches away.

A few quiet moments later, I looked at Zubin. "Actually, I wanted to speak to you too—that's why I tried to call. I wanted to ask if you noticed anything either during the train journey or before that, at camp. Did anything happen between Samir and Karthik?"

Zubin took a deep breath. "Actually, I think it did."

"What? When? What did you see?" My words came out fast and frenzied.

"It was sometime toward the end of the first week. We were on a hike that day. Each group took a different trail up the mountain. But there were a few places where the trails intersected. I was leading my group that day and around lunchtime, when I was hurrying to get to the midpoint intersection, I heard shouting up ahead. I thought someone might be in trouble, so I sped up, and then I heard arguing."

"Samir?"

Zubin nodded. "And Karthik. I arrived too late to hear what it was about, but Samir sounded pretty threatening— he seemed to be angry at your brother for 'meddling,' whatever that meant, and called him a hypocrite. Karthik didn't seem to be getting a word in edgewise. I've never heard Samir so worked up. Then there was a scuffle, and when I arrived, Samir had stormed off and Karthik was flat on his back, blood pouring out of his nose. When I helped him up, he said he tripped and fell and gave himself a nosebleed, but it was obviously connected to the argument. It must have been a pretty big deal, whatever it was."

"Aargh, Samir!" I sprang to my feet. "He just straight up lied to me. He said nothing happened at camp. Is this nothing?" Before I knew it, my feet were racing back toward the shelter. "I should just drag him into the police station right now."

"Lena, wait," Zubin called after me. "I know you're angry. I'd be angry too. But you need to calm down and think carefully before you do anything."

I slowed down and Zubin caught up with me.

"You talking to Samir again won't really help, will it?" He put a hand on my shoulder.

I stopped.

"Why don't you go home and talk to your parents first?"

I debated about what to do, staring at the shelter up ahead, nearly empty now. You and Samir weren't friends anymore. You fought at camp but covered it up. He switched rooms. He answered your phone when he shouldn't even have it—you should have it. He lied to me again and again. Meanwhile, you were still missing.

"Lena?" Zubin stepped in front of me.

"Yeah. You're right. I better go talk to Dad." I exhaled. "Thanks, Zubin. Thank you for talking to me and helping me earlier."

"No need to thank me. It's the least I could do." Looking a bit embarrassed, Zubin rubbed the back of his neck. "I just hope you find Karthik soon. He's a good guy. One of the best. Let me know if there's anything I can do to help, OK?"

"Actually, there is something I wanted to ask about the train journey." I suddenly remembered what Raheem had said.

"The train journey? Nothing out of the ordinary happened on the train. At least I didn't notice anything."

I nodded, expecting as much. "Raheem said that he saw someone wake up in the middle of the night, probably to go to the bathroom, but he wasn't sure who that was."

"It wasn't me." Zubin shook his head. "I was out like a light. I only woke up like a half hour before we reached Lamora."

"Oh. OK," I mumbled. That didn't really help me. If wasn't Zubin, it might've been you or Samir. It could be something or nothing at all, I couldn't be sure. But there was something I was sure of.

Samir was definitely hiding something.

And I had to find out what that was.

I thanked Zubin again and bid him a quick goodbye before running as fast as I could all the way home.

12

I raced up the stairs in our building two steps at a time.
I couldn't wait to tell Dad what I'd found out and rang the
doorbell impatiently.

Dad opened the door.

I hurried inside and he closed the door behind me.

"I need to tell you some—"

"Lena," he interrupted, towering over me.

"That liar, Samir is hiding—"

"See? This is what I mean. Look how she talks!" said a
voice from the living room. It was not Ma.

Dad stepped aside, and I saw Ma sitting on the sofa,
staring at her hands in her lap. And sitting next to her was
Samir's mom.

"Mrs. Pratap told us what happened," Dad said.

"I didn't do anything. It was Samir—"

"Quiet! Sit!" Dad ordered as if I were a puppy.

I clamped my mouth shut and followed Dad to the other sofa.

Ma didn't look up.

"I'm not here to cause any trouble," Mrs. Pratap said. "It is just not in my nature." Her brownish-red lipstick was smudged at the corner of her lips. "And what's happened to your family is just so tragic. But really, the way your daughter behaved today was shameful."

"The way I behaved?" I stood up. "What about Samir? Why did he fight with Karthik? Why does he have Karthik's phone? What is he hid—?"

"Upon my word! I won't stand hearing all these wild accusations about my son. He's a good boy. He is, my Samir. A very good boy." Mrs. Pratap shook her head vigorously.

"They are not wild accusa—"

"Stop." Dad gripped my arm. "Sit down, Lena."

I gritted my teeth and slid back onto the sofa.

"Mrs. Pratap tells us that you made a scene at soccer practice. You got in a fight with Samir and now you're saying that he has Karthik's phone?" Dad's voice was stern. "Explain yourself."

Forcing myself to calm down, I said quietly, "Last night,

I couldn't sleep, so I called Karthik's phone and I heard Samir's voice, so I—"

"That's a lie!" Mrs. Pratap squeaked. "Why would Samir—?"

"Mrs. Pratap, please wait." Dad held up his hand at her and then looked at me. "What do you mean you heard Samir's voice?"

"I mean . . ." I gulped as Dad's eyes bored into mine. "I mean . . . when I called, it was Samir who answered the phone."

Dad straightened his back. "What did he say?"

Uneasiness crept inside me. "He said . . . he said . . . He didn't say . . . much, but—"

"Are you sure it was him?" Dad asked sharply.

What if I'd gotten it wrong? "I heard it . . . I just know . . ." My voice faltered.

"This is unbelievable! She's just making things up," Mrs. Pratap screeched. "Really, Mr. Krishnan! See? This is why I had to come here personally. You must do something to control your daughter. This is just too much, I say."

Dad inhaled loudly, then in a quiet voice, he said, "Lena, apologize to Mrs. Pratap."

I felt as if someone had slapped me. Looking at Mrs. Pratap's smudged makeup, I forced myself to open my mouth. But the words simply wouldn't come out. Then I heard Dad say, "Oh, Nalini . . ." as he went over to Ma. He put a hand on her shoulder as tears dropped onto her lap.

My chin quivered as I looked at Ma. *How did it turn out like this? I was only trying to help. How did I end up making things worse again?*

"Look what you're doing to your poor mother." Mrs. Pratap tutted. "I can't even imagine what she must be going through. First to have a son like Karthik taken away and then for her daughter to do such shameful things . . ."

"Sorry," I blurted out, and ran from the room. I had left the apartment before anyone could say any more.

That Saturday afternoon, I walked and walked and walked, going nowhere. With every step I took, the lava of my thoughts bubbled and rose up in my head. By mid-afternoon, I found myself in Juna Bazaar amid throngs of people shopping for old, antiquey things. The market was buzzing. Alive. The vendors touted their wares, invited customers, pleaded with them to come back. The customers went from stall to stall, looking for a bargain, haggling with the vendors.

I remembered the last time we went there. "It'll be fun," you'd said. It had been you, me, and Ma—we had just had the kitchen redone, and Ma was looking for things to match the new color scheme. You persuaded me to come, and I sulked the entire way there. Then I complained the whole time while you helped Ma find what she wanted. You kept trying to involve me: "Look at this clock, El-Kay. Isn't it cool?" "What do you think of this Warli painting?" "I bet this bell is made of brass." I just responded by nagging you both to hurry up so I could meet Ayesha and my friends to go eat pani puri.

Now I left the bazaar and stood by the roadside, staring at the traffic, wishing I could turn back the wheels of time. A horn startled me, and I stepped back as a bus roared past.

I couldn't turn back time, but there *was* something I could do.

Ma and Dad were right to be upset about what had happened at the soccer shelter. But even though I'd hesitated earlier, I *knew* that the voice I heard on your phone was Samir's. Perhaps they weren't the ones I needed to convince.

I headed to the police station.

13

Busy attacking a piece of paper with his pen, Inspector Rana didn't notice me as I pushed the swinging double doors and stepped into his office from the corridor.

"What is this? Did you leave your brain at home today, Patil?" he barked at the old constable standing next to him.

"Sorry, sir. I asked Phule to do it, but—"

"Save your excuses. I don't want to hear them." Inspector Rana slammed the file shut and slapped it into Constable Patil's hand.

"Inspector Sir?" I stepped closer to the desk.

"What?" He looked at me.

"I have information about my brother," I said. "Karthik Krishnan?"

Inspector Rana narrowed his eyes. "You're the sister, right?"

"Yes, sir. I was here when my dad came to—"

"I remember. And I specifically remember asking your father to not let you come back here." He glared at me as Constable Patil shuffled his feet.

"Sorry about last time," I said politely. "Dad doesn't know I'm here, but I came because there's something I think you should know."

Inspector Rana grunted.

A thorn of discomfort lodged itself in my throat. I forced myself to swallow it and opened my mouth before I could lose my nerve.

"Sir, please, I have some information to help you," I said quickly. "I spoke to the boys who went to the same camp as my brother, and I found out that one of them, Samir Pratap, had a fight with Karthik. And I've been calling Karthik's phone and it's always switched off, but when I called late last night, it wasn't. And someone picked up the phone and I swear I heard Samir's voice. I know he has Karthik's phone, sir. He's hiding something. Please, sir." The words rattled out of my mouth like an express train speeding past a station.

Inspector Rana's face froze for a second. Then he nodded.

He believes me!

"Patil." He turned to face the constable. "Let's go, right now. Let's go talk to this Samir fellow." He stood up.

He *really* believed me. Soon, Ma and Dad and Mrs. Pratap and everyone would find out the truth. We'd find out what happened. We'd find you.

I stepped back toward the door, ready to go. But Inspector Rana didn't move. Neither did Constable Patil.

Thump!

Inspector Rana slammed the desk with both his hands. The files on the desk jumped and landed back with a soft thud sending little specks of dust flying in the air.

"You are trying to teach *me* how to do my job? You?" he yelled.

"But, sir—"

"What do think we do here, huh? Look, look at these." He slapped the files on his desk. "Murder, theft, robbery, arson, scams . . . The pile is taller than you! Do you think we sit here twiddling our thumbs?"

"I was only trying to help." My face flushed.

"Help?" He scoffed. "By asking us to chase down high-school boys because they *fought?*"

"But Karthik's phone—"

"Stop!" Inspector Rana growled. "I've heard enough of

your nonsense," he said, waving me away as he sat back down.

"But, sir . . ." Before I could say anything else, a booming voice called out to Inspector Rana from behind me. I turned and saw a big man with a flock of shocking white hair, dressed in khaki uniform stride into the room.

"Rana! What is this that I hear about problems with the chief minister's visit?" he yelled. His voice was so loud and intimidating that my feet moved on their own accord and started backtracking toward the door.

"Commissioner Sir!" Inspector Rana shot off his chair and scrambled around the desk to race to his boss's side. "It is just a small problem, sir. No need to trouble yourself," he said quickly.

"No need?" The commissioner scoffed. "Are *you* teaching *me* how to do *my* job now?"

I saw the inspector's face flush, and I felt a bit sorry for him.

"No . . . no . . . I would never dare to do that . . ." Inspector Rana shook his head forcefully. "Come, come, please. Sit down, sir." He gestured toward his chair. "Let me order some chai for you first, and then I will give you a full and complete update."

The commissioner grunted and headed toward the

chair as Inspector Rana yelled, "Patil! Go get two special chais. Jaldi, jaldi! Now!"

"Yes! Yes, sir!" Constable Patil said, already on his way to the door. He saw me still standing next to it and gestured for me to leave. I glanced at the inspector fussing about the commissioner. *It's probably best to wait outside,* I thought. But then again, maybe in front of the commissioner, Inspector Rana might *actually* listen to me.

I took a few steps forward, and mustering up my strongest voice, I said, "Inspector Sir! About Karthik's phone—"

"You!" Inspector Rana's face was stony. "You still here? Didn't I ask you to leave?"

"Please, sir, listen. If you trace his phone, you'll see it's with Sam—"

"Who's this?" The commissioner barked.

"No one. Nobody, sir. She's only a silly child," the inspector responded quickly, shooting me angry glance. Then his gaze shifted to the constable, who was standing next to me as if frozen.

"Patil!" Inspector Rana barked. "Why are you just standing there? Chai. Now! And take her away. If I see her here again, it'll be your neck on the line."

"Come, come, child." Constable Patil led me away quickly before the inspector could say any more.

Outside, in the corridor, I suddenly felt the weight of

a mountain on my shoulders. Constable Patil called out to someone to get the chai, then sat me down on a bench next to him.

"Why won't he listen to me?" I sniffled.

"Inspector Rana is . . ." He paused. "He can be a bit gruff. But he is really good at his job. In fact, he is one of the best."

"One of the best?" My words came out sharper than I intended.

"Yes, he has the best case-closure record in the entire city," the constable said calmly.

"Why hasn't he found my brother, then?"

Constable Patil sighed. "It's not that simple. We have hundreds of open cases on any given day and not near enough people to work on them. And the reality is that most missing children run away from home because they don't want to go to school or their families mistreat them or—"

"But Karthik didn't run away. He would never run away."

Constable Patil nodded. "Yes, it appears so. That's why we've done more than we normally would."

"But then, why is there no news still?" I said, feeling the weight pressing and pressing harder.

He looked at me kindly and said, "Look, I'll tell you

everything I know about the case. We informed all the local police stations in the neighboring districts. There were no First Information Reports lodged or reports of any accidents the night your brother went missing. We searched all the hospitals and morgues in the cities along the train route. No one matching his description has been found."

"But what about his phone?" I said, still feeling a glimmer of hope.

"We've contacted the phone network to trace his phone. But it can take up to two weeks. And if, like you said, his phone's been switched off, we may not find anything there, either . . ."

The mountain on my shoulders finally crushed me, and rivers of tears flowed down my face.

"I can only imagine how difficult this must be for you and your family," Constable Patil said. "I promise you, child, we're doing everything we can to find your brother."

His kindness only made me cry more.

"There, there . . ." He patted my shoulder.

We sat in silence until I'd calmed down.

"You should go home and be with your family," he said. "We don't want your parents worrying about you too, na?"

I nodded and thanked him and dragged my heavy feet slowly back home, wondering if I'd ever see you again.

14

I knew something was wrong as soon as Dad opened the door. He didn't ask me where I'd been. Or yell at me for what had happened earlier with Mrs. Pratap. Or even comment on how late it was.

"Dad, is everything OK? Is Ma OK?" I asked, ignoring the strange feeling at the pit of my stomach. Where *was* Ma?

He pursed his lips and indicated for me to sit down. So I did. The window curtains ruffled as a soft evening breeze blew in, carrying with it sounds from a TV blaring out of the apartment upstairs. Dad didn't say anything for several moments, and his silence wrapped around me like a prickly blanket.

"D-Dad?"

He sighed.

"Please, what's wrong?"

"Lena," he said finally in a voice that was quiet but steel-cold. "I'm only going to say this once."

I glanced at the corridor, hoping to see Ma. But she wasn't there.

"I understand how hard things are for you. But for your mother, they're . . ." He took off his glasses and rubbed his eyes.

"Dad, I know—"

"Let me finish." He held his hand up. "I know you think you're helping by questioning Karthik's friends and running around to the police station with your theories." He gave me hard stare. "But you are not."

Oh, no! Inspector Rana must've called him.

"In fact, you are making things worse. Today has been an incredibly trying day for me, but for your Ma, it's been . . . it's been devastating. The last thing she needs right now is to have to listen to the likes of Mrs. Pratap complaining about you or to worry that your shenanigans will insult the police or distract them from looking for your brother."

My chin trembled, and I looked down.

"Look at me, Lena." Dad's voice was stern.

I looked at him and felt something twist in my gut.

"We need to let the police do their job. We must trust them. If we interfere too much, it might actually make things worse. They might get distracted or start seeing us as a nuisance. Then, tell me, Lena, would that make them more or less willing to help us?" he asked.

I bit my lip.

"I know it's hard, but please don't go back to the police station." Dad put his glasses back on. "Also, we can't risk upsetting Karthik's friends and putting them off talking to the police. It might be best if you don't speak to Samir or any of Karthik's friends at all from now on. Let things calm down a bit, OK?"

My chin wouldn't stop shaking. *How would I find you then? You'd been gone for seven days.*

"OK?" Dad repeated. His face was a jigsaw puzzle of disappointment and worry and anger and fatigue. "Promise me."

My voice cracked as I said, "I promise."

Dad slapped his palms to his thighs and heaved himself up. "Dinner's in the kitchen. Eat up and go to bed." He left the room.

The curtains fluttered and the TV upstairs still blared as I thought about all the things I'd broken that day. I had to find a way to put them together again—and not break anything else. Especially not a promise. Wasn't it you who told me that breaking a promise is like breaking a heart? And I couldn't bear thinking about breaking Ma's and Dad's hearts again.

The TV upstairs switched off, and I sat listening to the silence for a while.

I was going to have to figure out a way to find you *and* keep my promise.

15

Sunday morning. Your favorite time of the week. I remember when you told me this, you said how much you loved the sound of the Sunday papers crinkling in Dad's hands. The aroma of biryani or bhajia or baingan bharta wafting from the kitchen as Ma cooked a special lunch. How you thought time passed differently, as if time itself was lazing around too. That's when I threw a cushion at you. "Stop being a bore!" I complained as it smacked you right in the face. And you chased me around the apartment until Dad yelled at us to pipe down. We crashed onto your bed, laughing, and then you said, "This, El-Kay! This is why Sunday mornings are my favorite!"

But that Sunday morning, time wasn't lazing around.

Dad had gone to the vegetable market; Ma was still asleep. The Sunday papers lay unopened, neatly stacked on the coffee table. No aromas wafted from the kitchen. That morning, time was in mourning.

I racked my brain trying to figure out what I could do next. I looked at my lists, and all I could think of was trying to find out who the "you" from your poem was. Then maybe I could find out from them what happened between Samir and you. But could I do that without breaking my promise not to speak to any of your friends? I decided to cross that bridge when I got there. I picked up the phone and called Ayesha.

"Hey, Ayu," I said.

"Hey. Still no news?" She must've heard it in my voice.

"No," I said quietly.

She paused, then asked, "How are you doing? And Uncle and Auntie?"

"It's hard, you know . . ."

"Yeah . . ."

After several moments of silence, I herded my wayward thoughts and said, "Can I ask you something?"

"Anything," Ayesha said.

"Fatima is in the year below Karthik, isn't she? Do you think she'll mind if I asked her something?"

"Of course not. Wait—I'll get her for you . . ." I heard

Ayesha yelling, "Fatima!" as she went to find her. "She's not here . . . Ah! Hang on . . ."

A moment later, I heard Fatima's voice on the phone. "Hey, Lena. How are you?"

"I'm OK. How are you?"

"Same old, same old, yaar." I pictured her nodding, her huge trademark earrings jangling. "Ayesha says you want to ask me something?"

"Yes . . ." Suddenly I felt as if I were grasping at straws. Still, I continued: "I wanted to ask if you know anything about Karthik's friends. I thought maybe toward the end of the year you might have noticed him hanging out with someone new or heard something or . . ."

"Nahi re. He's always with his same old gang, you know, Samir and the soccer crowd and all. And I've never heard any gossip about Karthik. Like ever. He's a scholar, yaar. Besides, after the fire in the chemistry lab, all anybody could talk about for the rest of the year was what happened. There were all sorts of weird and crazy theories like conspiracy ones, you know? It was hilarious. There was this one guy who said—"

"Fatimaaaaa!" Ayesha's voice in the background made me smile even though I'd run into yet another dead end.

"Sorry, yaar. Have you asked his friends? They might know something?"

"They don't know anything," I lied.

I heard Ayesha asking for the phone back and Fatima shooing her away.

"Hey! I know. If you are trying to find out about his friends and classmates and all, why don't you ask the teachers? They might know something."

A flame of hope lit in me. *That might work! And I wouldn't be breaking my promise.* Immediately, though, the flame started fluttering. "School's closed. How will I find them?"

"Just ask Principal D'Angelo. I'm sure he'll help. He likes Karthik. I saw him this one time, in front of the school noticeboard, congratulating him on his poem, which was published in *Indradhanush*."

"What?" *I couldn't believe my ears.*

Your poem was published in a national magazine. Actually published in an actual magazine! How could you not tell me, Kay-Kay? I hadn't even known you wrote poetry!

"Yeah, I know! Principal D'Angelo is really nice. He lives in a yellow bungalow at the end of the school lane. It's the one with a gulmohar tree in the front yard. You can't miss it!"

I thanked Fatima before quickly hanging up.

My head reeling with yet another of your secrets, I rushed to my room and got all your poems out. I laid them out on my bed and looked at them one by one, trying to figure out which one you'd had published.

I picked out my favorite one and read it again.

The Blank Page

The blank page calls to me
And I answer its call
We box, we wrestle
We whisper, we nestle
We create, we germinate
We sing duets and take turns being off-key
We drown ourselves in oodles of doodles
We play tic-tac-toe and sometimes I win
The blank page doesn't judge
It makes no demands, showers no praise
It just lies patient, in wait
So whenever the blank page calls to me,
I write.

Back in the living room, I scribbled a note for Dad saying, *Going to Ayesha's. Will be back this afternoon.* I put it on the coffee table next to the stack of unopened newspapers. I slipped on my shoes and headed out to find the yellow bungalow with a gulmohar tree in the front yard.

16

The iron gate creaked when I pushed it open. The gulmohar tree stood prettily in the veranda with its parrot-green leaves rustling in the wind, its orange flowers dancing in the sun. I walked beneath its shade toward the front door of the yellow bungalow.

I rang the bell, and a woman wearing a green sari hitched up high on her waist, opened the door.

"Yes?" she said, standing in the doorway with one hand on the door and the other on the doorframe.

"Is Principal D'Angelo in?" I asked politely.

"Who is it, Kanta?" called another woman's voice from inside.

"Madam, it is some girl," the woman at the door, who

must be Kanta, said, turning her head but staying where she was.

"What girl?" said the voice.

"Tell them it's Karthik's sister," I said. "The boy who's missing."

Kanta relayed back what I'd said without moving. I stared at my feet.

The boy who's missing. The missing boy. You.

"Oh-ho-ho. You poor, poor child." An older woman wearing a sunny blue floral dress shuffled up the passage toward me, while Kanta turned around and left.

"I'm Lena," I said.

"Yes, of course." The woman smiled. "Come inside, pet. Let's get you to my husband." She patted my shoulder.

I followed her into the living room. Embroidered cushions were placed neatly on a brown wooden sofa set. The coffee table was stacked with books, and a floor-to-ceiling bookcase filled one whole wall. Pictures and ornate objects hung on the remaining walls, which were painted a soothing ochre. Light streamed in through the big glass doors and lit up the room as if it were a painting. It was the kind of room that you'd instantly feel at home in, Kay-Kay.

Mrs. D'Angelo ushered me toward the glass doors and called out over her shoulders, "Kanta, bring us a pot of tea in the backyard."

We stepped into another painting. Potted cacti played hide-and-seek with rose and jasmine bushes. In a corner of the backyard, three trees—banana, coconut, and papaya—stood next to each other gossiping while a mango tree stood off to one side, lofty and grand, shading the patio, where Principal D'Angelo sat on a wicker chair reading a newspaper.

"You have a visitor, my dear," said his wife, beckoning me to sit. "One of your students."

Principal D'Angelo peeked over the newspaper and said teasingly, "And who might that be?" But all the humor in his voice disappeared the moment I introduced myself. He folded up the newspaper and put it on his lap as Mrs. D'Angelo sat down in the chair next to him.

"Is there any news yet?" he asked me.

I shook my head.

"The police have found nothing?"

"No, sir," I said.

He got up and started pacing up and down the patio. "Don't know why I'm surprised. The way they investigated the chemistry lab fire. Shambolic, I tell you. Utterly incompetent . . ."

A gentle breeze carried the scent of jasmine and roses to me as I sat quietly waiting for Principal D'Angelo, who kept pacing, shaking his head, and mumbling about the police and the City Council, to remember I was still there. Mrs. D'Angelo looked at me.

"Come sit down—you're making me dizzy," she said to her husband. "Look: Kanta's here with the tea."

Kanta set down a tray with a teapot and three cups on a small round table. She poured the tea into the cups and left quietly. Principal D'Angelo sat down and handed out the cups.

"I'm sorry, Lena," he said. "I get carried away sometimes."

"Only sometimes?" his wife teased.

"Oh, don't you start now!" Principal D'Angelo waggled his finger at her. Then they both smiled at each other and I couldn't help smiling too. It felt strangely comforting sitting in your principal's backyard.

"So, Lena, tell us why you came to see me today," Principal D'Angelo said once we all had a few sips of tea.

"Umm . . . Sir, I wanted to ask you about Karthik. You know him?"

The principal nodded. "Such a talent and what a lovely boy. I spoke to him not long ago when I heard about his poem being published. I already knew of his academic achievements, but hearing about his poetry made me even more proud."

Me too. I smiled.

Principal Sir smiled back and said, "But tell me, dear, what is it that you wanted to ask?"

I took a deep breath. "Karthik wasn't in any kind of . . . trouble, right?"

"Trouble?" Principal Sir thought for a few moments. "No, not that I know of," he said, shaking his head. "You are right to ask about it, though. Unfortunately, these days, there's always something. Usually, it's just kids playing truant or smoking or painting graffiti. But our school has had its share of serious things too. Everyone knows about the chemistry lab fire, of course, but there's been some other concerning incidents too. Like kids doing drugs or—"

"D-Drugs?" I asked, alarmed. "In the school?"

Mrs. D'Angelo slapped her husband's wrist. "Stop scaring the poor child."

"Oh, dear! I got carried away again, didn't I? I'm getting too old." Principal Sir shook his head. "I didn't mean to alarm you, Lena, and besides, you have nothing to worry about. I do not recall Karthik's name ever coming up in relation to these incidents. On the contrary, I never heard anything but praise from his teachers."

I nodded slowly, holding my teacup with both hands.

"But tell me one thing." Principal Sir looked at me intently. "Am I right in assuming that you think your brother's disappearance might have had something to do with school?"

"Yes . . . no . . . maybe . . . I don't know . . ." I said.

Principal Sir nodded. "It makes sense to explore all possibilities."

"That's why I've been looking for clues," I said, emboldened by his taking me seriously, "trying to find out about what happened before Karthik went to camp. Like when I looked through his things, I found out that he has a new friend but I don't know who that is. I thought maybe this person might know something. But none of Karthik's friends know about any new friend. So, then I thought maybe I could talk to other people from school. That's why I came here to . . ." My hands shook and I set my cup on my knees.

"Yes?" he said softly.

"I wanted to ask for the phone numbers of Karthik's teachers. I thought maybe they might've seen him hanging out with someone new or something."

Principal D'Angelo's eyes bored into me and I looked down at my teacup, expecting him to politely ask me to go home. Instead, he said, "That's a good idea, my dear. I doubt the police have even bothered speaking to Karthik's teachers."

My hands jerked, sploshing some tea on my jeans. *He doesn't think I am crazy. He is going to help.*

He looked through the open patio doors to Kanta, who was dusting in the living room. "Please get me the blue school attendance book and the black address book from the study," he called. Then he looked at me and said, "I doubt you'll get to speak to all his teachers. Most of them will still be on their vacations. And I need to get their permission first before I can give you their numbers. You understand, don't you?"

I nodded.

Kanta came out into the backyard with the books in her hand and handed them to Principal D'Angelo, who immediately started skimming through them. Then he got up and headed farther into the backyard, where he made some calls while I looked on anxiously, my foot tap-tap-tapping on the veranda.

"It'll be OK." Mrs. D'Angelo patted my shoulders.

I forced a small smile and forced my foot still.

A few minutes later, Principal D'Angelo came back and scribbled something on a piece of paper. He folded the paper in half and gave it to me, saying, "Phone numbers and addresses of Karthik's homeroom teacher, Mrs. Pillai, who also taught him physics, and his English teacher, Mr. Anjan.

They're expecting to hear from you. Godspeed, my dear."

I looked at the two kind faces in front of me, with their soft bespectacled eyes and wizened lines. "Thank you," I said, feeling a prickle in my own eyes.

"Not at all, my dear. I'm glad to be able to help," Principal D'Angelo said.

"We are praying for Karthik." Mrs. D'Angelo nodded.

I thanked them again and walked out of their backyard with a tender plant of hope sprouting within me. Back on the street, I unfolded the paper and looked at the two addresses. I glanced at my watch. I had enough time to stop by Mrs. Pillai's house on my way back home.

Your homeroom teacher lives on the third floor of an old building that has seen better days. There is no elevator, but I didn't care. You know how annoyed I get waiting for the elevator. I raced up the narrow, dark stairs and rang the bell, which had a stern-looking nameplate beside it that said

MR. RANGA PILLAI.

A woman with kohl-lined eyes and kohl-black, oiled hair opened the door.

"Mrs. Pillai?" I asked.

She nodded. "You must be Lena. Please come in."

"Yes, thank you." I stepped inside the small, neat living room, and Mrs. Pillai asked me to sit on the divan.

"Principal D'Angelo called and explained the situation," she said, sitting next to me. "You want to talk about Karthik?" She tilted her head to one side.

"Yes, ma'am," I said. "I don't know if you can tell me anything, but as you were his homeroom teacher last year . . ."

Mrs. Pillai nodded, and a faraway look crept into her kohl-lined eyes. "Karthik was my favorite of all last year's students. I know teachers aren't supposed to say this, but he was. I've been teaching physics for seventeen years, and I've never had a student like him. There is something special about him. And I'm not talking about his grades. It is his love of learning, his curiosity, just the way he thinks about things that is extraordinary. I can't believe that he's . . ."

As her voice tapered off, I remembered this one time when you and I were watching a rerun of 3 *Idiots* on TV. Out of the blue, you said, "El-Kay, I learned something amazing in physics today. I found out that light is both a wave and a particle, which are completely contradictory things. And then I found out that scientists now think that all matter in the universe is like light. You know what this means?"

When I didn't answer, you nudged me, and I replied cheekily, "It means you're a geek."

You grinned and continued: "It means, *we too* are made up of fundamentally contradictory things. It's almost like we are two different people at the same time."

I twisted my face in mock fascination, then punched you in the arm. Hard. You winced and asked me what that was for, and I replied, "I'm only proving you right. I'm your sister *and* your worst enemy. You made me miss the best bit, Kay-Kay! They were just about to find out who Rango really is."

You laughed and that made me even madder. I tried to punch you again, but you dodged, then you started goofing around and soon, your musings and my anger fizzled out in our laughter.

A physics geek and a poet.

Happy and sad.

Open and secretive.

"Are you OK?" Mrs. Pillai's voice brought me back to the present.

"Yes . . . sorry . . ." I said. "Please can I ask you something?"

"Of course." Mrs. Pillai smoothed her oiled hair.

"Did you notice anything about Karthik toward the end of year that was different, maybe unusual?"

"Different . . . not really, no." She shook her head. "I mean in the couple of weeks before school closed, he did seem quieter than his usual self. But then everyone gets like that before the final exams. He'd scheduled a meeting with me in the last week, but then he canceled it. I imagine it was some physics query that he managed to resolve by himself."

I nodded, trying not to feel disheartened by yet another dead end. I knew asking her about your friends would be a long shot, but I had nothing to lose. "Did you notice him hanging out with someone . . . new or from a different class?"

"I mostly saw him with Samir. Now, Samir, that boy!" Mrs. Pillai tutted. "I get a headache even thinking about him. Never know what he'll get up to next. I'm glad Karthik is his friend, though. He needs someone by his side helping him stay out of trouble. Your brother is good like that. Sensible. Considerate. That's why when the new boy joined midyear, I buddied them up."

My thoughts raced. "New boy?"

"Yes. Akash. Akash Khanna."

A name. I have a name.

"I'm so glad I chose Karthik. As I expected, he helped

Akash settle in—but it was later, when Akash got injured in the lab fire, that Karthik really outdid himself. He was one of the first to visit him at the hospital. He tried to help him keep up with his studies, too, but in the end, Akash had to have so much treatment that he couldn't even take the final exam, poor kid."

"What? Is he . . . is he OK now?" I asked. I'd had no idea it was your friend who'd been injured!

"Yes . . . yes, he's doing much better. Thank heavens. He still needs weeks of physical therapy, but he should make a full recovery." I breathed a sigh of relief as Mrs Pillai continued. "But it was just awful, what happened to him. Getting caught up in the fire and losing an entire school year as a result. Changing schools during the year is hard in itself without having to go through everything that he did. And don't even get me started on what happens when you're in an exam year. There's just too much pressure on kids nowadays. The board exams get harder by the year—it's all becoming just too competitive . . ."

Mrs. Pillai was still talking, but I had stopped listening. My brain was too busy figuring out how I could get Akash's number. Fatima! She could get it for me. I eyed the front door as Mrs. Pillai kept talking. Then I felt guilty for letting my attention wander.

I tuned in again to what she was saying, ". . . healthy and

happy. That's what should be the most important thing, but parents these days pressure the kids too much. There's always some or the other news report about the extremes students go to cope . . ."

Mrs. Pillai shook her head; she was getting quite worked up. "I myself have heard so many cases of children suffering from stress and anxiety and even depression." She paused. "I wondered sometimes you know, whether Karthik . . ."

"Karthik what?" I asked alarmed.

Mrs. Pillai's cheeks colored as she said quickly, "Don't worry. It's nothing, really. I just worried about Karthik sometimes. I know how hard he studied. I worried sometimes that he wasn't getting enough sleep or was feeling stressed or lonely perhaps . . . He tended to be quiet, you know. I'm not sure he'd have even told his friends how he felt."

Lonely. Is that how you felt, Kay-Kay?

One of your poems sprang to my mind.

A Lame Joke

How many letters do you need to write
to cure the lonely?
Only one

Cross out the n and write a v

And you're done.

Ha. Ha. Ha.

"I'm sorry if I upset you," said your teacher. "I tend to worry a lot about my students, all of them. I want them to learn, but I also want them to be happy. I'm always telling them to not work hard but work smart and if things get too much to take some time off, talk to someone. Our school has a full-time counselor on board, but hardly any of the students go to her. But I suppose it's a good thing if no one really needs her . . . Anyway I'm really sorry if I upset you."

"No, no." I blinked. "It's OK . . . Um . . . Is there anything else you think I should know about Karthik?"

She thought for a few moments, then shook her head and gave me a smile.

"Thank you for letting me speak to you," I said, standing up.

"Not at all." Mrs. Pillai stood up too, and showed me to the front door. "Please let me know if there's any news," she called after me.

"I will," I replied.

As I climbed down the stairs, my mind replayed the conversation and circled back to Akash. By the time

I reached the ground floor, there was a surge of energy in my legs. I ran all the way home, eager to call Ayesha. I sprinted through our building gates, whizzed past the ground floor lobby, and raced up the stairs to our floor.

Breathless, I stopped in front of our apartment door, about to ring the bell, not knowing in that moment that a nightmare was getting ready to unfold.

17

As I pressed the doorbell to our apartment, the elevator pinged behind me. I turned around and gasped as Inspector Rana and Constable Patil stepped out.

"Inspector?" I said, my voice barely audible. Before he could say anything, Dad opened the door and blinked in shock as he saw the three of us standing on the doorstep.

He glared at me, his face reddening. "Lena! What did you—?"

"Mr. Krishnan." Inspector Rana took a step forward. "We just bumped into your daughter. She didn't do anything."

A wave of relief washed over Dad's face. But it was

quickly replaced with dread, as he caught Inspector Rana's stony expression. Dad stood aside, and one by one, we made our way into the living room and quietly arranged ourselves on the sofas.

We sat under a dark cloud of silence for several long moments. Everything felt amplified, stretched out, in that void. The afternoon light was too white and bright, the whirring of the ceiling fan sounded like a revving motor-bike, and the room felt like an oven. A restless nervousness took hold of my body. My toes twitched, my fingers fidget-ed, my chin trembled.

Finally, Inspector Rana cleared his throat. He looked around the room and said, "Is Mrs. Krishnan home?"

"She's resting," Dad said quietly.

"I think you should call her, Mr. Krishnan."

"No, I don't think I should," Dad replied in a voice I barely recognized.

Inspector Rana rubbed his forehead. "Perhaps then the girl shouldn't be here?"

"*The girl* thinks she should," I snapped.

"Please just tell us what you came here to say," Dad's voice cracked. I gripped his hand.

Inspector Rana cleared his throat again and said, "I'm afraid, I have some bad news . . ."

I clasped Dad's hand tighter.

"A body has been found matching your son's description."

Time froze. My heart froze. I started falling into a black bottomless abyss, my arms and legs flailing, my mouth caught in a soundless scream.

Falling.

Falling.

Falling.

My heart jolted as someone screamed, "No! It can't be!"

I found myself back on the sofa. I was the one screaming.

Dad wrapped his arms around me, squeezing me tight, muffling my voice. "Shhhh . . ." he whispered in my ear.

"It may not be your son," Inspector Rana said quickly. "That's why you need to come to the morgue with us to identify the body."

"Shhhh . . ." Dad kept whispering to me. He only let go of me once we'd both stopped shaking.

"Mr. Krishnan?" Inspector Rana said.

Dad took off his glasses and rubbed his eyes. Then he looked at the inspector. "Morgue. Identify the body. Right."

"Are you all right?" Inspector Rana asked.

"What do you think!" I shot back. His jaw hardened, and Constable Patil fidgeted in his seat.

"It's OK, Lena," Dad said gently. "Sorry, Inspector. I'm fine. Thanks for asking. So. Morgue. Now?"

Dad was not fine. He was the opposite of fine.

"Yes, if you can. The sooner the better," Inspector Rana replied.

"Yes, of course. Of course," Dad said.

"We'll wait for you downstairs and . . . you can follow our jeep?"

Dad nodded as Inspector Rana and Constable Patil stood up and left quietly.

The clock ticked on and on and on as Dad sat, staring into space. Not moving. Not even blinking. His glasses were still in his hand, resting limply on one knee. His breath labored loudly. In. Out. In. Out.

I put a hand on his shoulder. "It's not him, Dad," I said.

He nodded and put his glasses back on.

"Right. I better wake Ma," he said, patting his knees. Then he got up and headed toward their bedroom.

"It's not Karthik," I called out again.

Dad didn't stop or turn around. But he nodded as he disappeared into the bedroom.

18

"It's not Kay-Kay. It's not Kay-Kay. It's not Kay-Kay. It's not Kay-Kay," I chanted under my breath in the back seat of our car as we followed the police jeep to the morgue. Ma was in the front, staring out the windshield, tears flowing down her cheeks. Every now and then, Dad would glance at her, hold her hand for a second, or pat her knee, or whisper her name.

"It's not Karthik!" I wanted to yell. It couldn't be you. Even Inspector Rana had said as much. But I didn't want to upset Ma and Dad any further, so I kept quietly chanting to myself till we entered the compound of the city hospital. Ma and I got out of the car and waited with Inspector Rana as Dad and Constable Patil drove to the parking lot.

The three of us stood uncomfortably as people passed

us by, going in and out of the hospital. An ambulance screeched to a halt in front of us, and a sudden flurry of activity followed. A small crowd gathered as the ambulance doors flung open and someone shouted, "Stretcher! Get a stretcher!" Two aides in white shirts and pants ran out to the ambulance yelling, "Move aside," "Get out of the way." They rushed to the back of the ambulance and reappeared, carrying a guy on the stretcher. He looked not much older than you. His clothes were soaked red, and he looked unconscious or . . .

I glanced at Ma, but she had not noticed the boy. She looked as if she were someplace faraway. I clasped her hand, but she barely seemed to register.

Constable Patil and Dad arrived a few moments later, and we headed inside the hospital, which smelled of disinfectant and sadness. We crossed the busy lobby, and Constable Patil indicated a staircase leading down to the basement.

"This way," he said.

Inspector Rana nodded curtly at the constable and said to Dad, "The girl can wait here."

"No!" I said.

Dad took my hand in his and looked at me. "Lena. Please."

I nodded slowly and headed toward the waiting area

while they all took the staircase. After a few moments, I doubled back to the stairs and followed them down, staying close to the wall. Pausing at the bottom step, I poked my head around the corner. They were all heading down a long, empty gray corridor. Halfway along, Constable Patil opened a door on the right and held it for the others. I counted to twenty, then stepped into the corridor.

As I walked, a strange heaviness seemed to drag me down. The discolored, stained walls cowered around me. The smell of disinfectant made my stomach lurch. With every step, the corridor seemed to stretch and stretch and stretch.

I tried to chant again. *It's not Kay-Kay. It's not Kay-Kay. It's not Kay-Kay.* But my mouth was dry and my throat prickled as I neared the door. I stared at the red letters above it. The U was dangling upside down.

MORG E

My hand shook as I reached out to push the door open. Just then an anguished scream echoed from the other side and I lurched back a step.

No! No! No!

I flung the door open and dashed down another corridor, crashing into Constable Patil. We staggered into a wall. Frantically, I scrambled to my feet, searching for Ma and Dad.

"It can't be him!" I said.

Constable Patil was saying something, but I couldn't hear it beyond my own garbled mush of words. "It's not Kay-Kay. It's not. It's not."

"Calm down." Constable Patil grabbed me by the shoulders to steady me.

Calm down? How can I calm down? I slapped his hands off and reached for the door again.

Constable Patil stopped me. "It's not your brother."

I froze. "It's not?"

He shook his head.

"It's really not?" I stared into his eyes.

"No, it really isn't," he said softly.

Relief wrapped me in a warm embrace, and tears flooded my face.

Constable Patil patted my back and said, "Let's wait outside."

"But I need to see Ma and Dad. I need to—"

"Let's give them a little more time, OK?"

Slowly, I nodded, and he led me back up to the waiting area, where he handed me a glass of water.

"What happened?" I drank a few sips. "That was Ma who screamed, wasn't it?"

Constable Patil nodded.

"I thought . . . I thought . . ." I sniffled. "Is she OK?"

"It was very hard on her. It would be hard on any parent," he said. "But you should try not to worry too much. I'm sure she'll be OK soon."

But he was wrong. He couldn't have been more wrong.

19

Ma looked even thinner in the pink hospital gown. She was sitting up in the hospital bed, her head propped up by a pillow. She had her eyes closed. Dad stood just outside the room, talking to the doctor.

After the morgue visit the day before, Ma had collapsed. A doctor saw her right away and had her admitted to the same hospital we had been visiting. She said that Ma was suffering from stress and exhaustion and it would be better for her to stay in for a few days. It had been hard to leave her, especially for Dad, who hadn't said much that night. But now we were back to visit on the dot when the visiting hours began.

As weak and worn-out as Ma looked, Dad didn't look great, either. I glanced at his tired, sagging face as he listened intently to the doctor. Suddenly, he exclaimed, "Thank God!" and the expression on his face relaxed a bit.

I breathed a sigh of relief too, hoping that meant Ma would be better soon. I handed her the magazines we brought from home. "I got these for you."

She opened her eyes and smiled but didn't look as she put them on the little table by her bedside.

"Lena?" she said.

"Yes, Ma?" I held her hand, looking into her eyes. The dark circles under them had darkened further even since yesterday.

"I . . . I . . ." she began but didn't finish. Instead, she patted my hand and looked out of the small window opposite.

"Can I get you anything?" I asked.

"Yes, actually, Lena," Dad said, coming back in the room. "Please will you get us some chai from the cafeteria?"

I nodded and stood up. "What did the doctor say?"

"She said Ma needs some tests."

"Tests? Why? What's wrong?"

"Don't worry." Dad patted my back. "They're only routine to see if Ma has a vitamin or iron deficiency. Nothing to be alarmed about."

I breathed another sigh of relief.

"Why don't you get us some tea?" He handed me some bills from his wallet.

Balancing a tray filled with two cups of chai, Marie biscuits, and a vegetable sandwich on one hand, I turned the handle to Ma's room. I pushed the door gently but stopped upon hearing Ma's sobs drifting out.

"Why is this happening to us, Arvind?" she cried.

"What use is thinking like that?" Dad replied softly.

"My darling boy. My Karthik. Why him? Tell me, why him?"

"Nalini . . . stop . . ."

"It's God's way of punishing me. I must have done something wrong. Why else would this happen? Why else would my boy go missing? Why else would I feel like I'm drowning . . . gasping for air . . . going under . . ."

I gripped the tray tightly. I couldn't move.

"You're not well, Nalini. You are not thinking straight," Dad said.

"I don't know what to do. I feel so helpless. We should be out looking for Karthik and instead we are here. All because of me."

"You just focus on getting better. The police will find Karthik. I know Inspector Rana is doing everything he can."

The tray in my hand shook a bit. Did Dad really think the police would find Karthik? Did he really trust Inspector Rana? I steadied my hands and was about to go in when Ma's voice carried toward me.

"This illness . . . this cursed illness . . . I thought I was better. But look at me now. I'm broken again—weak and broken. Just when I need to be strong—"

"It's OK, Nalini. It'll all be OK," Dad said firmly.

"How? When?" Ma cried in despair. "I'm tired of these relapses. How many times has it been since Lena was born. A child's birth is supposed to make a mother happy. Not make her ill."

What did she mean? What was she talking about?

"The past is in the past, Nalini. Just try to—"

"Everything was perfect when Karthik was born," Ma said fiercely. "My Karthik was perfect. And now he is gone. Everything is gone." She started sobbing again.

A knot appeared at the pit of my stomach as I took in her words. I gripped the tray tighter and looked down at the cups; the chai was getting cold. Steadying myself, I pushed the door open and finally stepped inside.

Ma had calmed down by the time we left her and was just nodding off again. Dad dropped me home before heading to work.

The net of Ma's words kept trying to trap me as I climbed the stairs to our apartment.

My birth had not been the happy occasion that Ma had hoped for or Dad had planned for. I had brought with me something that neither of them wanted or expected—Ma's illness. Suddenly, everything made sense. The reason why I was never good enough. The reason I always made things worse. The reason they loved you more than me.

I had to stop. I couldn't let the net ensnare me. Not after what had happened in the morgue. We'd managed to somehow stagger out of the deepest depths of the dark.

But there was only one way to climb completely out of the darkness.

The only way to make things right again.

I had to bring you back.

You've always been the light in our lives, Kay-Kay.

20

I turned the key in the front door. As the lock clicked open, I found myself thinking how strange it was that Dad hadn't even thought twice about giving me the keys to the apartment that morning. Remember how he always said that I was too irresponsible, that he simply couldn't trust me not to lose them?

Stepping inside, I wondered if he really trusted me now or was it simply because he had no choice? No time to worry about that now. I got my lists out of my bag and looked at them again. I realized that with all that had happened , I hadn't had a chance to call your English teacher yet: Mr. Anjan. I fished out the phone number that Principal D'Angelo had given me.

Mr. Anjan answered on the first ring as if he'd been waiting.

When I introduced myself, he said, "Tell me, Lena, how can I help?"

"Did you know or hear of anything unusual to do with Karthik before summer vacation?"

"Nothing out of ordinary, I'm afraid. I mean nothing that might have something to do with his disappearance," Mr. Anjan said.

I expected as much, but still I continued. "Mrs. Pillai said there was a new boy named Akash in Karthik's class. She said she'd asked Karthik to help him out."

"Akash?" Mr. Anjan paused. "You mean the boy whose arm was badly burned in the lab fire?"

"Yes. Was there anything that stood out about his and Karthik's friendship?"

"No . . . nothing that I can think of. I mean, Karthik was a good friend to him, as he was to everyone. He wasn't the sort to get into arguments or fall out with people—if anything he was the peacemaker. It was such a pleasure having him in my class, and his writing . . . well, it was simply a joy to read his work."

I bit my lip.

"Your brother has such a talent for words. That's why I recommended him to the young writers program."

"Young writers program?" It was the first I'd heard of it.

"Yes. It's one of the best s in our state, and it's very hard to get into. But Karthik was more than deserving of a place. He just needs to nurture his talent and keep working on his writing, and I know that one day he will accomplish his dream."

"Dream?"

"Yes, to become a writer. Didn't he tell you?" Mr. Anjan sounded surprised.

I mumbled, "No," wondering why you hadn't told me.

"That's too bad. I guess he feels a bit self-conscious. Writing isn't really *cool* with teenage boys, is it, now? Most boys his age are too busy trying to impress their friends, pretending that cricket and soccer are all they care about. I doubt Karthik felt comfortable even sharing it with his friends or classmates since most of them fit that category. But if I am being really honest, writing isn't considered cool by a lot of adults, either. It is a real problem in India today. Anything that is remotely creative is considered too airy-fairy, not practical enough, to be pursued. It's such a shame, isn't it?" Mr. Anjan sounded genuinely passionate.

When it was clear that there wasn't any more information that I could get from him, I interrupted him politely and brought the conversation to a close by thanking him and promising to let him know if there was any news.

After we hung up, I sat next to the phone for a while, wondering why you felt you had to keep your dream a secret. Was it because you felt it was something you couldn't or perhaps shouldn't do? I remembered one of your poems, talking about dreams. I hadn't fully understood it the first time, but now I suddenly thought I did. I dug it out and read it out loud to myself, the words rolling off my tongue with an easy rhythm and an uneasy force. Your words.

Past, Present, and Future

Young man, remember
that backs broke to pave your way
young man, don't forget
that shoulders sagged to take your weight

Young man, recognize
their pain, their sacrifice will always be greater
so young man, don't speak
of trivial travesties, of dreams that don't matter

Young man, realize
your past was a gift

> your present, a duty
> and your future, young man,
> is a debt, unpaid.

I'm sorry, Kay-Kay. Sorry that you felt like that. Sorry that I didn't even know. I've always thought that your life was perfect. Everything seemed to go your way, come easily to you. It never even occurred to me that you dream of doing something other than what Dad expects of you.

As I wondered about your dreams, my eyes drifted to the empty space in the middle of the living room wall studded with your awards and certificates. The empty space that Dad had proudly proclaimed to have left for your national scholarship award even before you sat the exam. Suddenly at that moment, I remembered how small your face looked, how quiet your voice sounded when you told us that you'd failed the exam. Ma couldn't believe it and Dad looked as if he was hit by a truck. I, too, was shocked to hear it but I won't lie, a tiny part of me was actually a bit glad. I felt like less of a failure myself, you know. I'm sorry Kay-Kay. I wish I'd hugged you then and said, *What's the big deal?* to Ma and Dad. I wish I'd checked if you were OK. I wish I'd cheered you on like you always do me.

Right then, I promised myself, that once you came back, I'd make you tell me everything—about your poems and your dream and the young writers program, about what happened between you and Samir, about how you felt about failing the scholarship exam—everything. And we'd have no more secrets. Ever. Whatever happened, we'd muddle through it together. Because, like Nani always said, that's what families do, right? And I want to do that for you.

Then I got back to work, scribbling all over my lists.

THINGS I'VE FOUND OUT

1. Nothing was found in the train other than your backpack.
2. Your phone is missing.
3. You and Samir are no longer best friends.
4. You like poetry and you like to write poetry.
5. Samir and you had a fight at camp and he switched rooms.
6. Samir has your phone.
7. The police have found no more clues.
8. You canceled a meeting with Mrs. Pillai not long before the exams.
9. You became friends with a boy called Akash Khanna, who was new last year.
10. You got a place on something called the young writers program.
11. You dream of being a writer.

When I finished, my mind kept circling back to Akash. Who was this guy? What did you talk about? What if he knows something? I couldn't shake off that thought, so I rang Ayesha again to see if Fatima could help get Akash's phone number for me. She promised to check and ring me right back.

My foot tapped incessantly as I stared at the phone, willing it to ring. The clock ticked on, but Ayesha didn't call. Frustrated, I headed to the kitchen to make some chai. I added grated ginger and let the tea boil on the stove for a few minutes longer to make it extra strong. I ripped open a new package of Parle-G and took four biscuits out. Back in the living room, I sat surrounded by my chai and biscuits and my lists and your poems as if they were obedient courtiers waiting for their orders.

The phone rang just as I was taking a sip of the hot, strong chai. I nearly spilled it all over the coffee table as I rushed to pick up the phone. Ayesha gave me Akash's number and I added it to my lists. Turned out that Fatima knew Akash's sister. What are the odds, huh? But I didn't have time to dwell on that. The main thing was that I had Akash's phone number in my hand.

Now what?

As I looked at it, the sword of my promise hung over my neck. I had promised Dad I wouldn't speak to any of your friends. The phone number taunted me, laughed in my face.

Did I dare call it?

Ma's thin figure in the pink hospital gown popped up in my head. Dad's broken voice shook in my ears.

No. I couldn't, I wouldn't, break the promise.

So now what?

I felt like a mouse trapped in a maze. The more I pored over my lists, the more flustered and frustrated I got. I just couldn't find a way out. Fury spilled out of my eyes. I threw cushions against the walls, kicked the coffee table, and ripped up the lists. The rage left me empty, and I finally crashed on the sofa, staring at the wreckage around me for several moments. Then I picked myself up and put everything back.

I taped the lists back together, and as my fingers smoothed the crinkles, an idea started forming in my mind.

Something definitely happened on the train.

Something probably to do with Samir.

The only way left for me to prove that was to find some evidence.

The only way to find evidence was to go to where it all began.

To the place where you were last seen.

21

I was so charged up with the idea of retracing your last train journey that I could barely sit still.

I thought about what I already knew.

You boarded the train safely at Margao Junction. The camp coordinator had confirmed it. Samir, Raheem, and Zubin had all said they'd last seen you around 9:30 p.m. Even if I didn't trust Samir, I had no reason to think Raheem and Zubin would lie about that.

You disappeared sometime after 9:30 and before the train arrived at Lamora.

I looked up the ERS–Lamora Express route online and found that at that time of night, the train is scheduled to stop at only two stations in between: Kolar Station at 10:05

p.m. for three minutes, and Aravali Junction at 2:20 a.m. for twenty-five minutes.

I looked up the two stations, poring over train and bus timetables, making notes as I went along. I found a bus that leaves the Lamora Central Bus Depot every morning at ten a.m., getting to Kolar at six p.m. Perfect! I could get to Kolar Station, do some investigating there, and then get on the ERS–Lamora train at 10:05 p.m. I could even get off at Aravali Junction, where the train halts for about half an hour. If I was quick, I could speak to the stationmaster and a couple of other people and get back on the train before it left and be back home in Lamora the next morning.

But I needed money.

I rushed to my room and got my secret stash out from the bottom drawer of my desk—all of the birthday and Diwali and Rakhi money that I'd been saving for the last two years to buy a smartwatch, like the one my friend Renu has. Remember what Dad said when I asked him for one? He said it was "colossal waste of money." But as I clutched the bills in my hand, I was actually glad for once that Dad hadn't bought me the watch. Otherwise, I would never have saved up the cash. I counted the money. I had enough for both the bus and train tickets. There wasn't much left over.

But that was all I had and it would have to do.

I listened to the sound of laughter coming from outside. Soft evening light shimmered in through the window, painting an abstract picture on the tiled floor of our living room. A brisk breeze blew in, ruffling the curtains. I felt a strange calm come over me. The restlessness was gone, replaced by something deeper, stronger.

I looked at the piece of paper in my hand.

Hold on, Kay-Kay. I'm coming.

22

I could hardly sleep that night.

The nervous energy built up again after Dad came home. I was relieved to hear that Ma was doing better and would be back home in a couple of days. And I was really glad that she was getting the rest and care she needed. But I won't lie, Kay-Kay, a guilty part of me was also secretly glad that she was in the hospital, because it made things easier for me. I'm not sure I would've had the nerve to do what I was about to do had Ma been home.

All through the evening, the crazed horse of my thoughts kept racing ahead to the next day and I had to keep reining it back. To making chai. Helping Dad with dinner. Eating. Doing the dishes. All the while keeping my mouth shut. Luckily Dad was so lost in his own thoughts, he didn't seem to notice my nervousness.

When I could finally escape to my room, I flumped on my bed, letting out a long sigh of relief. A little later, I took out the photo of you and me from the photo frame on my desk. The selfie of us at Bee Falls. Your arm is slung across my shoulder, and you are smiling into the camera while I'm making a face at you.

Do you remember that vacation in Pachmarhi? Ma was tired of climbing up and down the paths to the waterfalls. And Dad had had enough of the mosquitoes and hawkers. But I wanted to go to Bee Falls. I'd been wanting to go there from the moment I heard how the sound of the waterfall is like that of a thousand bees humming. So you convinced Dad and Ma to let us go by ourselves, promising to be careful. They listened to you, as always. And we went and played games and sang songs and collected leaves and pebbles as we hiked to the falls. And when we got there, we stood in front of the cascading water, laughing and taking silly pictures as its spray tickled our faces. And then we screamed, loud and long into the water's roar.

My fingers hovered over the photo for a few moments before I slid it into the folds of the newspaper article about you and put them in the front pocket of my backpack. Next to them I placed my lists. I took your poems and the compass out of my desk drawer and put them in the backpack too. I didn't need any spare clothes, but then I thought it might get chilly on the train, so I packed my navy hoodie. I carefully set out a pair of blue jeans and a red T-shirt for the next day. Then I went to bed. But sleep was a mirage that tricked me all night.

Every time I woke up, I saw you.

You teaching me to ride a bike. Not letting go till I'd say so.

You racing me in the park. Running slowly so I could catch you.

You breaking the fancy chocolate bar in two. Giving me the bigger half.

You changing the topic when Dad was on my case. Dousing the fire.

You sneaking into my room past our bedtimes, playing cards with me. Letting me win.

You smiling, laughing, running, talking, playing, reading . . .

You. You. You.

23

The next morning, I made extra-strong chai. My hands shook as I poured it into two cups. Dad looked at me quizzically for a moment before taking a cup from me. While he got dressed to go work, I packed his lunch, then arranged his briefcase, lunch box, and water bottle neatly on the coffee table.

Dad rushed in, adjusting the blue striped tie that did not go with his yellow shirt and brown trousers. As he put his shoes on, strands of gray hair flopped onto his glasses. I felt a pang in my chest. *It must be so hard for him.* He needed me. He relied on me. And I was about to lie to him. But then I thought of you.

Finally, he gathered up his things from the coffee table and headed to the front door.

"Call me if anything . . ." he said over his shoulder.

"Dad?" I called after him. "I . . . I . . ."

"Yes?" He turned back, and his tired brown eyes looked at me through the thick lenses of his glasses.

I felt my chin tremble. I didn't trust myself to speak. So I hugged him on the doorstep.

"It'll all be OK, Lena," he whispered, patting me gently on the back.

"Yes, it will," I whispered back, letting him go. He nodded and I waved at him as he got in the elevator.

I closed the door and stood leaning on it for a moment.

Then I called Ayesha. I told her about my plan and asked her to cover for me if Dad called. She protested at first. "It's too dangerous. What if something bad happens?" I forced myself to ignore the fluttering in my stomach and calmly explained my plan step by step. "See, I've thought of everything. Please, Ayu . . ." I pleaded. To which all she said was, "But, Lena . . ." That's when I told her about what Constable Patil told me and about what happened at the morgue and about Ma being in the hospital. I asked her, "If you were in my place, what would you do?" She went quiet for several moments and then she asked me to promise her that I'd be careful. And I did. Then she asked me to call her immediately if anything happened. And I did.

Then I wrote a note for Dad and left it on the coffee table.

Dear Dad,
I've gone to Ayesha's for a sleepover. We checked with her mom. Auntie said it was OK. I will be back tomorrow morning. Sorry—I tried to tell you this morning, but you were in a rush.

Please don't be mad.
Love,
Lena

I packed two sandwiches, a bag of chips, a chocolate bar, a banana, and a bottle of water in my backpack. After checking my wallet one more time, I left for the bus depot.

24

The Central Bus Depot was a hive of activity. Just like it was the last time we went there, when Ma insisted on taking us both to Maugad to visit her old school friend.

Remember that trip? I was so angry because Ayesha and Renu and Mira were all going to the movies. And instead of having fun with my friends, I was being forced to go on a day trip to meet another one of the aunties. And as I expected, when we got there, Ma's friend gushed all over you as Ma listed your achievements while I sat there stuffing stale, dry biscuits into my mouth, feeling every bit like a part of the furniture.

But right then, as I stepped inside the bus depot, I thought how I'd happily turn into a sofa or a chair if only you'd come back.

Dusty green buses roared and revved around me, pulling in and out of two long rows of parking bays. At the far end of a waiting area was the ticket counter.

A bus pulled into bay 9 and I got caught up in the rush of passengers clamoring to board it. Behind me, I heard the bus conductor yelling, "Ticket! Ticket!" and people shouting, "Stop pushing!" and "Get in a line!" I paused for a moment to catch my breath, then headed to the ticket counter.

I stood at the back of a long line, glancing at my watch. *How could it only be twenty-five minutes before the bus left?* There were at least thirty people ahead of me. Sweat stung my eyes as my foot tapped on the floor. My watch raced ahead, but I'd hardly moved at all.

Someone yelled "Go back in the line!" and suddenly people started shouting and shoving one another. A policeman standing nearby ran up, cracking his cane on the floor and yelled, "Stop that!" He grabbed a tall scruffy guy by his collar and shouted at the scuffling group to move aside. The line shortened and I said a little prayer.

As the minutes ticked by, my T-shirt began to stick to my back. I took my backpack off and slung it in front of me. A large group of people left the ticket counter together, smiling and chatting, and within a couple of minutes, I found myself at the front. The counter was run by a man who had a toothpick poking out of the corner of his mouth. An older man in gray shirt and pants stood behind him.

The man with a toothpick tilted his chin up at me.

"One child ticket for Kolar, please," I said, sliding the money through the small window on the counter.

"No tickets," he said. Then looking over my head, he yelled, "Next!"

"But . . . but . . ." I panicked. "There's a bus that leaves at ten o'clock."

"Yes. There is a bus, but there're no spaces left. Now go. Next!"

Someone behind me started pushing to get to the counter. I refused to budge.

"Please, sir!" I said, "I only need one ticket. Only one child ticket. I cannot miss the bus. Please, sir."

The toothpick man tutted. "Arre, yaar . . ."

The man in gray put a hand on the toothpick man's shoulder. "Are you traveling alone?" he asked me.

I nodded.

"Where're your parents?"

"My mother is . . ." I sniffed. "She's in the hospital." I don't know why I told him the truth. It just came out.

The man looked at me for a second and said, "I'm the driver of the ten a.m. to Kolar. There is an extra seat in the driver's cabin. We don't usually sell it to customers. But you can have it you want."

"Yes, please. Thank you! Thank you!" I couldn't believe my ears.

"OK. See you in bay 3 in five minutes," he said.

"Yes. Yes, Uncle." I reached for the ticket that the tooth-pick man slid toward me.

When I reached the bus, it was full and ready to leave. The driver waved me into his cabin at the front and I took my place at the small seat in the corner. Relieved, I hugged my backpack as the bus reversed out of the bay and thundered out of the depot. As it hit the highway, leaving the busy streets of Lamora behind, the driver sang a song I recognized, from some old black-and-white film, and it reminded me of Ma. The bus hummed on the road and the wind whistled in through the window, and soon I drifted off to sleep to the sound of the driver's singing.

Someone was shaking my shoulder gently, saying, "Wake up."

I rubbed my eyes open. "Are we there?"

"No." The driver laughed. "We're stopping for lunch. For half an hour. There's a bathroom down at that end," he said, pointing out of the window.

"OK." I looked out and saw a small bus station with a restaurant next to it.

"You'll be OK?" asked the driver, opening the cabin door.

I nodded as he stepped down. A moment later, he poked his head back through the door and said, "What is your name? In case you're not back in time and I have to call you?"

"I'll be back in time," I said.

He pushed back strands of gray hair flopping onto his forehead. Just like Dad.

"Lena," I said. "My name is Lena."

"Don't go far, Lena." He smiled, his eyes creasing in the corners.

I smiled back.

Back on the road, the driver chatted to me about his three children as I ate my lunch—the sandwich and banana. Two boys, naughtier than monkeys, he said, and one girl, the apple of his eye.

"Sonal." He said her name as if it was the sweetest word under the sun. He told me he had high hopes for her. She was the one, he said, who would do him proud. Then he went back to his singing.

I looked out the window at the flat brown landscape

split in half by the straight black highway. The scorching summer had squeezed all life out of the land. It cried out for the monsoons, still days away. My thoughts drifted like the wind, hot and dusty. I thought of the driver and of Dad—both fathers who expected their children to do them proud. And I thought of the driver's daughter and of you—both children who had to live up to those expectations. That reminded me of something you'd written, and I got the wad of your poems out of my backpack. That's right; it was even called "Expectations."

Expectations

concentrate

don't slouch

stand up straight

eyes on the prize always

luck is not chance

burn the midnight oil

move heaven and earth

toil don't complain

turn every page

go the distance

take no prisoners

no one remembers the second best

race ahead
race to the top
race against time
leave all else behind

I race race race
I leave behind my dreams
my words
my whole self.

I looked out the window again. As the brown landscape whizzed past, my thoughts whizzed too. I never realized how hard it must be for you to be the top student, to keep acing exams. The way Dad expects you to just do it, the way Ma talks about you so proudly, the way your teachers use your name as a shining example—it must all be a bit too much, right? Like you can never make a mistake, never disappoint, never fail. I don't know why I've never thought of this before. But now your poems, your beautiful poems, Kay-Kay, are making me think, helping me understand . . .

"We're here," the driver announced.

"We are?" I jolted in my seat, dropping the poems on the floor. I'd nodded off again.

"Right on time." The driver smiled, helping me pick up the scattered papers.

I quickly put them in my backpack and followed him out of the empty bus. My shoes thumped on the dusty ground as I looked around. The bus station was much smaller than Lamora Central Bus Depot. It only had six bays, and the main building had a sloping tiled roof, like the kind you might find on houses in the villages.

"Is someone coming to collect you, Lena?" the driver asked, looking concerned.

"Yes. Yes. My dad is coming," I said quickly. "Where can I wait for him?"

The driver pointed at the main building. "You'll be OK?"

I nodded slowly, feeling a pinch of sadness. "Thank you for letting me sit in your cabin."

"No need to thank me. I hope your mother feels better soon." He pushed back the gray hair flopping onto his forehead. "I'll tell my Sonal about you. When she grows older, I want her to be confident and brave like you."

He smiled as he walked away.

I headed inside the main building and found a phone booth, where I made a quick thirty-second call to Ayesha to let her know that I'd arrived safely. I needed to save every rupee I could. Then I asked for directions to the train station. A short walk later, I found myself standing in front of another building with a sloping terra-cotta-tiled roof, with the words

KOLAR RAILWAY STATION

glinting in the evening sun.

This is where my search for you truly began.

25

The station lobby was small and deserted. On the left, there were newspaper and snack stalls. On the right was the ticket counter, and beside this was a big wooden blackboard with arrival and departure times listed on it. I crossed the lobby and found myself on one of the two train platforms. Hardly anyone was about.

A loudspeaker crackled, "Attention! Attention! The Superfast Mumbai–Kochi Express will now be passing through Platform 1. Please do not cross the tracks. Attention! Attention!" A shrill train whistle sounded, followed by the train thud-thudding through the platform. I closed my eyes and mouth as dust and litter flew in the air. Moments later, the train was gone, and the chocolate wrappers and scraps of paper and plastic settled back onto the platform.

I adjusted the straps of my backpack and walked down Platform 1. A man dressed in black jacket and white pants came out of an office.

"Sir," I said, "are you the stationmaster?"

He turned to look at me. "Hahn," he said looking annoyed.

"My brother, he's missing, and I wanted to ask you . . ."

"Me? Why? Shouldn't you speak to the police?" He began to head toward the entrance lobby.

"I know, sir." I followed him. "But my brother went missing on a train. And I wanted to ask you—"

"Then you should speak to the railway police," he said over his shoulder.

"I just have some questions about the train he was on."

"Questions about trains?" The stationmaster paused in front of a door to the men's toilets.

"It'll only take two minutes. Please, sir."

He grunted. "I don't understand why a girl like you is going around questioning me about trains. How will that help? And besides, I am busy today. I don't have two minutes. I don't even have one second." He pushed the door open. "Come back to the office tomorrow morning if you want. Maybe that slacker Bijoy will have time to answer your questions."

"Please wait," I said. "I can't come back tomorrow . . ."

The door banged shut behind him.

What now?

I looked up at the slice of sky between the two platform roofs, creased crimson and pink by the evening sun. A picture-perfect sky. The kind of sky you'd probably write a poem about.

Feeling a bit lost, I returned to the lobby.

"Oi!" called a voice.

When I looked around, I saw a boy who looked about eight or nine years old, leaning against the empty chai stall. He was dressed in a dirty yellow shirt that was a bit too small and raggedy khaki shorts that came to his knees. He whistled at me, not in a bad way, but in the way people whistle to hail a rickshaw.

I pointed at myself. "Me?"

He nodded and I walked over to him.

"Chai?" He poured hot tea from an aluminum kettle into a small glass.

"Yes, thank you," I said, feeling a sudden surge of tiredness in my limbs.

"Biskoot?" He gave me a small package of Parle-G.

"My favorite," I said, ripping open the package and offering him some.

He smiled, taking a couple and cramming them in his mouth.

"What did you want from that grumpy, khadoos stationmaster?" he asked, his mouth full.

"I had some questions about a train." I took a biscuit and dunked it in the tea.

The boy scoffed. "He doesn't know anything."

"What do you mean?"

"He's number one kaamchor. Sits in his office doing nothing but barking orders, sipping chai, not even lifting his little finger."

"Oh."

"But I know who does know things." He thumped his chest.

"Really?"

"Yes. I can tell you." He leaned in and said in a low voice, "But it'll cost you."

"Cost me?" I asked, puzzled.

"Yes. My services are not cheap." He puffed up his chest.

My shoulders sagged. I knew I wouldn't have enough money left once I'd bought my train ticket. "How much?" I said.

He tilted his head up, closed his eyes, and tapped his temple with his finger. Then he looked at me and said in a very serious voice, "Two packages of Parle-G, one Bourbon, and one cashew Good Day."

I almost choked on my biscuit.

"It's not a joke!" he huffed, crossing his arms over his chest.

"Sorry. Sorry," I said. "I'll do you better, I'll even throw in a bag of chips. How does that sound?"

"Sacchi-mucchi, God promise?"

"God promise."

I unearthed the bag of chips from my backpack as he went around the stall to get the biscuit packages. I paid him for the biscuits and tea and handed him the chips. He put the money in a little tin box and the snacks in a flimsy plastic bag.

"Stan the Man, at your service, miss," he said, grinning from ear to ear.

I smiled. "Well, Stan the Man, who can answer my questions about trains?"

"Follow me." He led me out of the lobby onto a platform, where we turned left, passing a waiting room with a big padlock on its door. We continued along the platform until the end, where it sloped down toward the tracks, and kept on walking, passing the green signal lights, and finally came to a halt in front of a thin two-story building that looked like a cardboard box.

"Madhu Kaka," Stan hollered.

"Stan?" A bearded face peered down from a second-floor window.

"Kaka, please will you help this miss?" Stan pointed at me. "She has some questions about trains. Grumpy, khadoos stationmaster didn't help her at all. She gave me chips."

Kaka laughed, his long white beard swaying. "Yes, why not?" he said. "Come on up—the door is open."

Stan grinned at me, then said, "Bye," and turned to leave.

"Aren't you coming?" I asked, feeling suddenly uneasy at the prospect of going inside alone.

"Nah!" he said. "Jaggu will have my hide."

"Jaggu?"

"The chai-wallah. My boss. I've already been gone for too long."

"Oh."

"But don't worry. Madhu Kaka is the best! He likes Parle-G too." Stan smiled, waved at me, and ran back to the station.

I waved back and pushed the door open.

Stan was right. Madhu Kaka was the best. He'd been a signal guard at Kolar Station for forty-two years. Can you believe that, Kay-Kay? Forty-two years of sitting alone in a
tiny room in a cardboard-box building, with only a tele-
phone, the road crossing gate levers, a signal lantern, and
green and red flags for company. But the loneliness didn't
seem to have made him sad or bitter. If he was sad about
anything, it was his failing eyesight. He showed me his
register, in which he'd meticulously logged the arrival and
departure of all the trains that had ever passed through
Kolar Station.

I turned to the page dated May 13 and traced my finger
down through Madhu Kaka's train log. My finger stopped.

There it was staring at me, another dead end:

ERS–Lamora Express
Arrival—*On time*
Departure—*On time*

I inhaled.

Your train drew into Kolar and left three minutes later,
as scheduled. Nothing out of the ordinary. No delays.

No problems. Nothing. As I studied the log, Madhu Kaka leaned out the window, waving the green signal lantern. The cardboard-box building shook as a train rattled past.

I exhaled.

After waiting for Madhu Kaka to log the entry for the train just gone and work the levers to open the train crossing gates, I thanked him and left.

I headed back to the ticket counter and bought my Lamora Junction ticket. As I put the change and ticket away, I saw Stan signaling me from the chai stall across the lobby. A thin, tall man with coiffed black hair, Jaggu, I presumed, was behind the counter, pouring tea into the aluminum kettle. Stan was making hand gestures, trying to tell me something, but I couldn't understand.

"What is it, Stan?" I yelled.

His eyes went wide, and he shook his head tightly. Jaggu looked up, about to say something. But before he could, Stan said, "I'll bring your chai to you by the waiting room, miss." Then he made a face at me, puckering his lips and raising his eyebrows.

"OK. Thank you!" I called back cheerily.

As I was heading for the waiting room, out of the corner of my eye, I spotted Jaggu glaring at Stan as he poured tea in a cup. I sat on a bench on the platform. Stan arrived moments later.

"Sorry for making you buy another cup of chai, miss. But Jaggu wouldn't have let me come otherwise." He handed me the cup.

"It's OK," I said, sipping the sweet, gingery tea. "I needed it, anyway."

"Madhu Kaka helped?"

"Yes, he did." I sighed.

"But it didn't really help?"

"No," I whispered.

Stan sat down next to me quietly as flies buzzed around my chai and mosquitoes circled around us both. He clapped his hands to shoo them away. The dark curtain of night fell, and the electric lamps on the platform came on. Stan looked up at the beaming yellow light and said, "My mother used to say, even in the darkest of dark, the light of hope burns bright. You only have to look deep within your heart."

His face was awash with the sad glow of happy memories.

"Thank you," I said softly.

"For what?" he said, jolting back to his normal self.

"You know, for—"

"Fleecing you?" He winked.

I chuckled. "I shall recommend your services to all my friends."

He laughed. A giggly laugh that got us both going. Afterward, I showed him your photo. Your train had only stopped here for a few minutes, but just in case you got out, if there was anyone who'd have noticed, it would've been Stan.

He stared intently at the photo as if it were a museum artifact. Then slowly, he shook his head. I asked him if he recalled any incidents on that night or the next morning. He shook his head again. I nodded, putting your photo back in my backpack. It was such a pity and not only because it was another dead end—I'd expected as much. But also because, Kay-Kay, you'd have loved meeting Stan.

26

My watch said there was still an hour before my train. I ate half of my second sandwich, saving the other half for Stan. I walked up and down the near-empty station, wondering if I should ask Jaggu or the newspaper guy, if they'd seen you too. But the newspaper stall was closed, and when I saw Jaggu eyeing me suspiciously, a strange feeling gnawed at the pit of my stomach. You told me once that our instincts are messages our guardian angels send our way to guide us on the right path. I listened to my guardian angel. Besides, I didn't want to get Stan in trouble.

Back on the bench outside the waiting room, impatience simmered inside me. I was eager to get on the train and onto to the next stop—to the junction where the train always stops for twenty-five minutes. If I was to find any-thing, I was sure to find it there.

I swatted at some mosquitoes whining in my ears as another train rattled past. A few people arrived with their luggage and made their way to the handful of benches scattered on the platform. Stan went up and down, hand-ing out and collecting teacups. I hailed him over.

"Have this." I held out the half sandwich.

Stan eyed it but didn't say or do anything.

"Don't you like sandwiches? I made it myself."

Stan didn't reply but kept looking here and there while sneaking glances at the sandwich.

"All right!" I let out an exaggerated sigh. "I'm too full to eat it and if you don't want it, I guess I'm going to have to throw it away." I stood up and took a couple of steps toward the trash can. The next moment, Stan snatched the half sandwich from my hand and, cramming it into his mouth, raced off.

I couldn't help smiling as I sat back down. I looked up at the night sky, a thick blanket stretching into the un-known, sprinkled with shining stars. We never get to see the stars like that in the city. But out there, in a small town with no brash city lights dimming their glow, the stars shone so bright.

Do you remember that time when Dad didn't let me

go on the school trip to Coorg? I was so angry, I kicked the coffee table, knocking it over and breaking Ma's favorite teacups. That night, as I cried into my pillow, you tiptoed into my room. With a finger on your lips, you took my hand, and we snuck up to the roof, where you'd put up a makeshift tent. The city turned into a jungle, our building into a tree, and the tent became a machan, where the two of us hid—intrepid adventurers ready with our binoculars, on the lookout for predators. Then the machan transformed into a spacecraft tearing through galaxies as some stars exploded into supernovas blinding us and others imploded, sucking us into black holes. Early the next morning, the yoga class aunties found us sprawled out there on blankets. They tutted and shook their heads and we just laughed as we gathered up our stuff.

Goose bumps appeared on my arms now. I put my hoodie on and then took out your poems, shuffling through them till I came to this one:

Carl Sagan Said

On starry nights
I think of what Carl Sagan said.
"The cosmos is within us.
We are a way for the universe to know itself."

So the key to unlock all the mysteries
must be inside
all of our infinite selves.

The loudspeaker crackled, and people stood up and got ready to board the Lamora-bound train. I looked at my watch; it was just after ten p.m. As the train's whistle sounded in the distance, I stood up too, your poems still in my hands. Then a sudden gush of wind arrived from nowhere. Dust flew in my eyes, my hair flew in my face, and your poems . . . your poems flew out of my hand. I ran after them, scrambling, one poem being dragged under the bench, another one getting plastered to the waiting room door, and the others flying even farther away.

The train was at the platform. People yelled, "Hey, open the door!" "Quick! Get in!" "Grab the bags!" as they scrambled onto it. As the train whistled again, I saw it start moving, gathering speed by the second. I watched as it left the platform, which was strewn with pages etched with your beautiful poems.

I had no choice, Kay-Kay.

I wasn't going to lose them too.

27

I gathered up your poems, counting them again and again to make sure they were all there and held them close to my chest for several moments before putting them back in my backpack. I looked around the deserted platform, lit only in patches by the electric lamps with shapeless shadows lurking around. No other passengers were left. No new passengers would arrive for there were no more trains until the morning. I was alone. Utterly alone in this dark, desolate place.

A machine-gun fire of questions rattled holes in my brain. What am I going to do? Where will I sleep? What will Dad do when he finds out?

"Miss?" said a voice as a hand touched my arm.

I looked up and saw Stan's face.

"Are you OK?" he said gently.

I bit my lip not trusting myself to speak.

"Why aren't you going home?"

"I . . . I missed my train . . ." I whispered finally. "I have nowhere to go."

Stan nodded, then looked up and down the platform. Not a soul was in sight. Suddenly, he gave a dramatic spin followed by a little jump, landing right in front of me, his hands on his hips. Then puffing out his chest like a superhero, he said, "Fear not, miss. Stan the Man is here."

Despite everything, as I looked at Stan's skinny figure, I couldn't help but smile.

"Come," he said, beckoning. He led me down the platform and around the side of the waiting room. In a flash, he hopped up onto a window ledge.

He put a finger on his lips and nodded silently. A faint creaking sounded from inside the waiting room as Stan pulled at a barely visible string hanging down the side of the window. As the string went taut, he gently pushed the window's shutter open. He jumped inside, first onto a bench underneath the window and then onto a faint yellow rectangle glowing on the waiting room floor. He landed soundlessly, like a cat.

"Come, quick," he said.

I got up on the window ledge and followed him inside. A musty smell hit my nose as he closed the shutter behind us. The yellow rectangle on the floor disappeared, leaving us standing in the dark. But there was nothing scary about it. In fact, the darkness was comforting. It seemed to say, *You're safe. You can relax now.* And I did, relief coursing through my veins.

Click. Stan was holding a flashlight under his chin, which lit up his face. He rolled his eyes, twisting his face and said in a deep voice, "I am Stan the Gho-o-ost."

I gave a small smile, thinking how lucky I was to have met him.

"Do you think this is funny, silly human?" Stan widened his eyes and twisted his face even more. "Do you?"

"No, sorry, Stan the Ghost, sir! Please don't kill me," I said in mock fear. The least I could do to repay his kindness was to play along.

"Ghosts don't kill, *pagal* human! We steal your so-o-oul."

"Please spare me, Stan the Ghost, sir. Don't steal my soul," I pleaded.

Stan lifted his arms in the air and walked around like a zombie. Then he lurched at me and growled. We both burst out laughing, covering our mouths with our hands, trying not to make too much noise. Once the laughter faded, we flumped onto the bench with our backs to window. I took Stan's flashlight and flicked it around the small, sparse waiting room. Two other bare wooden benches hugged the walls, and on the fourth wall was a door leading onto the station platform, locked from the outside.

"Is this where you sleep?" I whispered as my mind flashed images of my room back at home. My bed with the flowery bedspread. My desk stacked with knickknacks. My wardrobe stuffed with clothes.

He shrugged. "It's not so bad. It's a hundred times better than sleeping on the platform or on the street."

"I'm sorry."

"Why're you saying sorry, miss? It's not your fault."

"I just feel . . ."

"It's OK. I feel the same way sometimes when I look at Gimpi or Ashok. They work in the market stalls and have to sleep on the street. Sometimes . . ." Stan paused for a couple of moments. "Sometimes I feel like telling them about this," he said, gesturing around the room. "But then we might get caught and Jaggu would have my hide and grumpy, khadoos stationmaster would kick me out . . ."

Stan looked so small, hunched next to me in his dirty, tattered clothes. I felt a pang in my chest.

I took the chocolate bar from my backpack and nudged his shoulder.

"Chocolate?" I said.

His eyes twinkled and a smile danced on his lips. "You'll share it with me? Sacchi-mucchi, God promise?"

I handed him the chocolate bar. "It's for you," I said. "Sacchi-mucchi, God promise. Consider it a tip for your excellent services."

Stan's face lit up like a Diwali lantern. "Thank you!" he said, taking the chocolate bar and slipping it into the pocket of his khaki shorts. Then he crossed the room and pulled a plastic bag out from behind the bench. Inside it was a thin sheet, which he handed to me. "You can have this tonight if you want. I'm used to the cold."

"I'm all right. This hoodie is warm," I assured him.

We settled in for the night. Stan on the bench by the window, and I on the opposite one. I rested my head on the backpack, trying to get comfortable on the hard, cold bench. Stan switched off the flashlight and started humming. The tune reminded me of a lullaby Ma used to sing. The one about the moon and the cup. You remember? As I listened to Stan's gentle humming, my mind filled with a jumble of thoughts and worries and fears—about Ma and Dad and you, of course, you. But thankfully my body was too tired and when sleep called her gentle call, I instantly replied.

28

"**M**iss, wake up."

I tried opening my eyes, but my eyelids felt like they were sewn shut. "Hmm . . ." I mumbled.

"We have to go, miss." Stan shook my shoulders.

"Yes . . . yes . . . sorry," I said groggily, sitting up. I opened my eyes, stretching them as wide as I could. The room was still dark, but slivers of light slipped in from underneath the window shutters and around the door. My watch said it was quarter to six in the morning. As I struggled to wake fully, Stan looked at me with the alert eyes of an animal sensing danger. He glanced at the door and said, "It's almost time for Babu, the cleaner, to open the waiting room. If he finds out we slept here, he'll go running to the grumpy, khadoos stationmaster."

"Sorry," I said, hauling myself up. My body felt stiff all over, and I groaned picking up my backpack.

Footsteps sounded outside. And whistling. Stan's face went white as he rushed to open the window. I hurried to it too. The waiting room door went *clunk* as Babu yanked it from outside, probably putting the key in the lock. Stan was already on the window ledge. He put a finger on his lips, nodded at me, and stealthily jumped out.

Quickly, I followed. Stan stood by the window, gesturing for me hurry up. I jumped and landed with a thud.

"Koi hai? Is someone there?" called a gruff voice.

Stan slapped his forehead. He put his fingers underneath the window shutters and pulled at them gingerly. They clicked shut just as the waiting room door slammed open.

"Come quick," whispered Stan, leading me around behind the room.

"Phew!" Stan leaned against the wall. "Lucky escape. Or else today toh, I would've been roasted like tandoori chicken . . ."

"Sorry."

"Happens, miss. Even to the best of us." Stan smiled at me. "Come, let's go."

Early morning mist hovered in the air as we slipped through the gap between the back wall of the waiting room and the bushes behind. Stan led me into a small alley, and a few minutes later, I found myself standing in front of the station entrance. I didn't want to get Stan in any more trouble, so I thanked him and said goodbye, promising I'd see him later. As he headed back into the station, I went in the opposite direction.

The town was still waking up when I found myself back at the bus station. I should've been almost home by now, with evidence or at least a clue to help find you. But there I was, still in Kolar, with two choices before me: either catch the ERS–Lamora Express that night and continue with my plan or take a bus back home to Lamora now.

The sun peeked over the bus station, its golden rays sliding down the sloped roof. I took a deep breath and stepped inside. There were hardly any people around as I made my way to the restroom. But in the time it took me to freshen up, a few people had gathered around the ticket counter. As I neared it, my legs shook.

Take the bus. Go home. Just what do you think you'll find on the train, anyway?

I gripped the straps of my backpack tightly trying to steel myself against my wobbly thoughts. I found myself taking the backpack off and reaching into the front pocket. My fingers touched upon cool metal and I took out the compass, placing it on my palm. I watched the compass needle sway this way and that, and when it finally settled, I knew exactly what I had to do.

You got me the compass. It has to show me the right way.

I walked out of the bus station, not even glancing at the ticket counter.

Through the now-thinning early morning mist, warm rays of the soft yellow sun lit up my path like spotlights on a stage. Soon I found myself in a market. Stall owners clanked shutters open and arranged their wares. Shopkeepers cleaned the front porches of their shops, dust flying as they swept. The gingery aroma from a chai stall made my stomach grumble. After a quick breakfast of tea and biscuits, I searched the market for a phone booth. I decided to wait till mid-morning before calling Dad, knowing that he's usually in meetings then and wouldn't pick up his phone. I left him a voicemail saying I would stay over at Ayesha's again. I thought about ringing Ayesha too, but I knew this time she wouldn't go along with it. And I didn't want to get her in trouble.

I felt awful about lying, Kay-Kay. But what else could I really have done?

A little dusty path only wide enough for one car stretched before me. On either side were small houses painted in lively colors, their tiled sloping roofs shading the path. A bicycle bell tinkled behind me, and I stepped aside. A man on a red bicycle raced past, yelling, "Watch out!" at a group of little children playing on the path up ahead. They sprang out of the way and then chased after him, yelling and laughing.

Soon the air felt heavier on my skin and a salty scent mixed with a whiff of dried fish prickled my nose. The sea was close. I picked up the pace as houses tapered off, palm trees appeared, and dust gave way to sand.

I found myself standing on a strip of golden beach dotted with colorful fishing boats. Beyond it, blue-gray water shimmered, stretching all the way to the horizon. A salty breeze whistled, tickling my neck and ruffling my hair.

It looked like the beach from my dream. Any moment now, I thought, I'd see you laughing and running in the sand. Sunlight shimmied in my eyes as I saw a figure in the distance walking toward me.

My heart missed a beat. *Is that you?*

Blink! The figure turned into a fisherman headed for his boat.

I slumped down onto a rock under the shade of a swaying palm. I felt as if someone had poked a hole in me and let all the air out. My eyes watered as I took in the splendor around me. But what good was cool, golden sand if your feet weren't here to leave their marks on it? What good were dancing waves if you weren't here to dance with them? What good was anything at all if you weren't there?

Wrapping my arms around my knees, I let the tears flow down my cheeks.

Later, after my tears had dried, I sat quietly, listening to the wind whistling over the lonely beach. I found myself reaching for your poems once again, like some kind of comfort blanket, sifting through them till I found one that fit my mood.

A Love Letter

Blue Blue
infinite blue
Blue Blue
ancient blue
I am a speck
smaller than a grain of sand
I am just a boy
not yet a man
I am no different
from countless others
who've stood at your feet
who'll swim in your arms

• • • •

But, Blue Blue,
My heart, it swells
with the swell of your waves
It ebbs
with the ebb of your tides
It snarls
with the snarl of your storms
It hums
with the hum of your ripples

Blue Blue,
Deep beautiful blue
how my heart loves you.

A salty breeze danced around me as I carefully returned your poems to my backpack along with my shoes and socks. Then I rolled my jeans up to my knees and walked toward the lapping waves to meet the Blue Blue you love so much.

29

Dusk and I arrived at the same time. As I entered the railway station once more, I glanced at the ticket counter. Guilt and worry poked my mind at the thought of my near-empty wallet. I didn't have enough money left to buy the ticket a second time. I'd pushed away the nagging worry all day, but there was no escaping it now—I was going to have to travel without a ticket.

Just stay out of the ticket checker's way. It'll be OK.

I headed to the chai stall, where Jaggu was stirring tea in a pot on the stove.

"Where's Stan?" I asked.

Jaggu's eyebrow arched. "What do you want him for?"

"Umm . . . nothing . . ." I said, feeling the chai-wallah's piercing gaze hovering on my face.

"You're that girl from yesterday, right?"

"No . . . No, I'm not," I said quickly.

"No?" he scoffed, narrowing his eyes.

I took a step back, pulling at the straps of my backpack.

"So, you're here again *alone*. I wonder *why*." He looked me up and down with a sinister smile on his lips.

"I have to go!" I shuddered, retreating from the stall.

"Word of advice before you go." He smacked his lips. "There are many wild animals in the jungle. Lions, tigers, cheetahs, you name it. A lamb like you, out alone by itself, had better watch out."

I looked straight at his black eyes. I wanted to yell at him. Slap him. Tip the chai pot on him. Instead, I gritted my teeth and walked away, listing my top ten films under my breath: "One, *Taare Zameen Par*; two, *Dangal*; three, *Chak De! India*; four, *Secret Superstar* . . ."

"Watch out, little lamb!" Jaggu called after me. But I was already on film number eight and Jaggu didn't matter anymore. I headed for the waiting room.

You know, Kay-Kay, as I looked at the padlocked door, a strange mix of emotions stirred in me. My mind swam back to the night before. What would've happened had Stan not helped me? Stan the Man, a little boy with a big heart.

The thought of saying goodbye to him stung my eyes. I sat down on a bench, wondering how it was that someone I'd known for only a day could make me feel like that.

As the evening wore on, the sky turned from saffron to slate. Trains whistled and rattled past. Dust flew in the air and settled back on the platform. Every so often, my eager feet would take me back to the entrance lobby and my eyes would dart around, looking for Stan. But every time, I returned to the bench with heavy feet and downcast eyes.

Where is he?

The sun hid and the stars came out to seek. They didn't find Stan, either. The loudspeaker blared, announcing the arrival of the ERS–Lamora Express. I strapped my backpack on my shoulders and got ready to board the train. There was no way I was missing it again. As its whistle sounded in the distance, its form grew bigger and bigger, clattering on the rails. And then with a screech and a clang, it came to a halt in front of me. I grabbed the cold metal door handles and climbed onto the train. But I didn't go inside. I turned around and remained standing at the door.

A cold gush of wind blew in my face and I inhaled sharply. My eyes swept up and down the length of the platform as I willed Stan to appear. But all there was to see was a long, half-lit, empty space. A minute later, the train whistled and jolted into motion. Inch by inch, it gathered speed, leaving the station behind, blurring in the darkness. I waved at it long after it disappeared from my view, long after even Madhu Kaka's green lantern stopped shining from his cardboard box.

I never did see Stan again.

30

A gentle, cool wind blew through the window as I stood listening to the thutut-thutut, thutut-thutut of the train for a few minutes. Then, feeling calmer, I finally made my way into the train. Immediately I bumped into a man who was passing through the vestibule to the next carriage.

"Oho! Careful!" he said, steadying himself.

"Sorry, sorry!" I noticed he had a clipboard in his hand and was dressed in black jacket and white pants. Oh, no!

"Which compartment?" he barked.

I gulped. "What?"

The ticket checker tutted. "What's your compartment number?" he asked loudly, his face a picture of irritation.

"Umm . . ." Like a cyclist pedaling uphill, my brain

worked furiously to concoct an answer. I couldn't say the number of the compartment that he was about to go into. But I hadn't noticed what number it was when I got on the train.

"Arre, yaar! Don't waste my time!" he said. "Show me your tick—"

"S5, my compartment is S5." I blurted out the number of the compartment you had stayed in the night you disappeared.

He grunted. That was it, I thought. *What will he do when he finds out I don't have a ticket?*

"OK, go," he said. "I'll come later to check your ticket." Then he stomped around me as I thanked my lucky stars.

Quickly then, I headed into the next carriage, which turned out to be number S3, and walked along the narrow, dimly lit passageway past the compartments, which I knew contained six sleeping berths each. I slowed my pace, peeking inside the compartments as I passed. It wasn't that late, but with nothing much to do on the train, most people were already lying on their berths. Some were scrolling on their phones, some shifting and turning, trying to get comfortable, while others looked fast asleep already.

Compartment after compartment, it was all the same. Dim lights, closed windows, people lying on their berths. Occasionally, I'd spot a compartment with people still up, having a late dinner or playing cards or chatting in low voices. As I neared S5, I felt a tingle of nervous energy. I couldn't be sure, but there was a chance that this was the actual train on which you'd traveled. There was a chance that I was about to see the actual berth where you slept.

As the train rattled on, I made my way in the hazy yellow light of the passageway. Outside the third compartment, I looked at the berth numbers: 19–24. You'd had a lower berth by the window. I peered inside and saw a large man sleeping on berth 21, your berth, with his head nearest the window. His enormous stomach, half covered by his shirt, tumbled up and down with his whistling breaths. Aside from this, it was otherwise quiet. I waited a few minutes, then tiptoed inside.

Trying not to make any noise, I looked around the tiny space, straining my eyes. Over and under the table. Around the windows and the berths. I was looking for clues, any signs that you'd been here—perhaps something of yours that you'd accidentally left behind or a message that you'd scribbled on the wall or something like that. But it was hard to see anything, and with all the berths occupied by people, I had no chance of finding anything at all really.

A wave of fatigue swept over me.

What was I thinking, anyway? What was I going to find that the police didn't? And in the dark too!

The man on berth 21 grumbled in his sleep. I stepped back hastily, and as I did, I stumbled on some shoes in the middle of the floor. I gasped and lost my balance, falling backward. My arms flailed as my hands tried to find something to hold on to. They landed on a dangling bedsheet.

Thud!

I was on the floor, the bedsheet in my hand, and a split second later, it was mayhem.

"Who's there?" someone yelled.

The compartment lights flashed on, blinding me.

"What are you doing?" A woman glared at me from a middle berth, her hair resembling a bird's nest.

"Umm . . . nothing . . . sorry . . ." I mumbled, getting up, trying to slow down the hammering in my chest. Others woke up now too, sitting up on their berths.

"Why do you have my bedsheet?" the woman said loudly.

I glanced at the peach fabric, still in my hand. "Sorry—I was only . . . I didn't mean to." I stood up to hand the sheet back.

Whump! A small purse landed on the floor.

The woman looked at the purse, her mouth shaped into an O. Then she pointed at me and yelled, "Thief!"

"What? No . . . no . . . no!" I said, aghast, my eyes darting between the purse and the woman. But it was no use; the woman kept yelling, "Thief! Thief!"

People began to jump down off their bunks. I bolted.

"Stop! Catch her!" someone yelled.

As I raced down the corridor, compartment lights came on one by one and footsteps thumped behind me. Panic swirled inside me as people poked their heads from the compartments, asking, "What's going on?" "What's happening?"

Someone grabbed my backpack, yanking me backward, yelling, "Got her!" I grunted and lunged forward desperately, loosening their grip. And then like a sprinter at the starting blocks, I launched myself and raced to the end of the carriage. I ran through the narrow passageway between the restrooms, then through the connecting vestibule into the next carriage, and kept running through the dimly lit corridor.

"There she is!" someone yelled.

As I glanced back, a compartment light came on and I saw two men chasing me. The one in front was wearing a lime-green checked shirt.

I kept running to the end of the carriage and onto the next one. And the next one and the next, not stopping even when all had fallen quiet behind me. When I reached the last carriage, I slipped into the restroom and locked the door.

Out of breath, I swallowed a lungful of air, and the rank toilet smell hit me. I rushed to open the small window and gulped in the cool, fresh air for a few moments. Then I glanced at my watch: 11:18 p.m. Still three hours to go till Aravali Junction. I waited inside the restroom, alert to any suspicious sounds.

After about half hour of hearing nothing but the train's rattle and the wind's whistle, I opened the door slowly and peered out. Not a soul was in sight. I stepped into the dimly lit vestibule and snuck a quick peek down the corridor. No compartment lights were on. No one was awake. Relieved, I sat on the floor of the vestibule. Sleep weighed on my eyelids. I tried to stay awake, but as one moment turned into another into another, the train's thutut-thutut turned into a lullaby and the vestibule into a rocking chair.

31

A shrill whistle startled me awake. Sleep lingered on my eyes as I stood up and looked out the door, wiping drool off my chin. The train rattled past a big board with

ARAVALI JUNCTION

written in black. I thanked Lord Ganesh that I had been sleeping lightly and hadn't missed the stop altogether. As the train slowed, I glanced behind me. No one seemed to be getting off at this end of the carriage. I pressed the handle down and pulled the heavy door open. Cold wind gushed in, and I shivered. The platform was covered with an eerie yellow light from the station's sodium-vapor lamps. I had exactly twenty-five minutes before the train departed at 2:45 a.m.

I was fully awake and I was ready.

As soon as we came to a halt, I stepped down off the train and had a quick look around for the ticket checker. The platform was quite busy for the time of the night. Tea and snack stalls were open and clumps of people were scattered around, sitting on benches or their suitcases. A small group got down from the next carriage and dragged their luggage out onto the platform. Two sahayaks, dressed in trademark red shirts and white pants, ran up to help them.

With no ticket checker in sight, I headed toward the station concourse, wondering what to do next, when I caught a flash of green out of the corner of my eye. I looked and my breath got caught in my throat as I saw a man in a lime-green checked shirt standing a few paces away. The man who'd chased me on the train. He yawned, stretching his arms in the air, and walked toward the tea stall. I put my hood up and my head down and headed in the opposite direction toward the footbridge connecting the platforms.

Don't look back.

I climbed up the stairs, patterned by a mesh of light and shadows.

Stay calm.

At the top of the footbridge, I paused and glanced both ways. With no lamps, the bridge was lit only in patches by the light from the platforms below. I walked along it until I could see the whole length of the platform below me. I watched a group of people carrying suitcases and bags, walking toward the footbridge. Others hovered by the train doors, smoking cigarettes, while others gathered around the tea stall. Lime-green shirt guy was one of them.

My watch said there were only twenty more minutes before the train left. I couldn't go back to the platform while he was still there. And even if I did, what was I really going to find in twenty minutes?

The foolishness of my plan slapped me hard.

I hardly have any money left.

I've found nothing. Not a shred of evidence. Not a single clue.

The weight of my failure dragged me down.

I should get back on the train while the coast is clear.

I should go back home before I really mess things up.

Gripping the railing tight, I squeezed my eyes shut. The cold metal sent a shiver through my body, and suddenly a scary image appeared in my head.

An image of you. In the cold. In the dark. Alone.

I gasped, and my eyes flicked open. By the time the group with all the luggage appeared on top of the footbridge, my mind was made up.

No! I can't give up. I won't give up. I will stay here and keep looking. I have to.

I followed the group a few paces behind, knowing they would be heading to the station exit. We climbed down the stairs to the farthest platform. The stalls were open there too, but it was far less busy. Other than the passengers making their way toward the exit, there was hardly anyone around. Picking up the pace, I looked for the waiting room. Walking quickly down the platform, I passed the stationmaster's office. At the exit by the office, the sahayaks were asking the sleepy-eyed ticket checker to hurry up checking passengers' tickets.

I hurried past them, hoping to find the waiting room before the platform emptied, and as I did, I tripped and fell. My knees thumped into the hard concrete and my hands scraped in the grit. A little cry escaped my lips, and at that exact moment I heard a loud howl behind me.

My mouth went dry. I stood up shakily and slowly turned around.

A man with a long, dirty beard and thick, knotted hair stared at me with bloodshot eyes.

My stomach tightened into a rock.

He leaned in, opened his mouth, and let out a foul-smelling scream.

I froze, as if I were faced with a roaring bear.

"Go back to sleep, Sharabi Baba!" someone yelled impatiently from farther down the platform.

Sharabi Baba clamped his mouth shut and stared at me.

Not a single muscle in my body moved.

He shook his head from side to side, and his long, dirty hair slapped my face. Then he turned around and abruptly walked away as if nothing had happened.

Some moments later, when the shock had worn off and my body had relaxed, I realized the waiting room was right in front of me. As I peeked through the door, the ERS–Lamora Express sounded its goodbye whistle.

It'll be OK. Just one more day. I'll be OK.

The waiting room was much larger than the one where Stan slept and was occupied by about a dozen or so people in various states of sleepiness. I spotted a couple sleeping in a corner. The man's head rested against the wall and the woman's head rested on the man's shoulder. I tiptoed over to them, taking my backpack off my back and slinging it across my front. Quietly, I sat down in the empty seat next to the woman. Anyone looking at us would assume we were together.

Hugging my backpack, I rested my head against the wall and let myself fall asleep.

That night, as I slept in the threadbare safety of a pretend family, I dreamed of Ma in her pink hospital gown. Only she wasn't in the hospital room where I'd visited her. She was in the morgue, with the *U* dangling upside down over the entrance. She banged on the door, screaming your name over and over and over again: "Karthik! My Karthik!" I reached out to her, but as soon as we made contact, she crumbled like chalk and disappeared.

I woke up gasping for air. A man sitting opposite looked at me quizzically. I went red and looked away. Bright daylight shone upon the cream walls. There were far more people in the room than there had been the night before, although the seats next to me were empty. The couple, my pretend family, was gone, and it was time for me to get going too. I tried to bat away the speeding balls of thoughts hurtling through my head as I left my temporary refuge.

What now? How would I get home? What would I say to Dad and Ma?

I headed to the restroom and tried to freshen up as much as I could. I hadn't showered or changed since I'd left home two nights earlier. I ran my fingers through my hair and looked at the face staring back at me from the mirror. It looked like me. Brown eyes; a snubby nose; short, frizzy hair. And yet the face looked nothing like me. It's difficult to explain, Kay-Kay. As I stood there, I felt as if the real Lena were somewhere else. And the one standing there was a stranger.

The door to the restroom clanged open, and a couple of college girls walked in, chatting loudly. They glanced at me, crinkling their noses. I splashed water on my face and hurried out.

Sharabi Baba, the old man, was sprawled like a bird on the platform beside a concrete column, snoring loudly. I walked past him toward the footbridge thinking how in the morning light, he didn't look scary at all. Just sad.

I swerved around the steady stream of people going in and out of the station and raced up the stairs. From atop the footbridge, I saw rows of rails fanning out, gleaming in the lemony light of day, interspersed by the dark concrete of the platforms. How different the view looked then. Somehow more alive. More promising. Feeling hopeful, I climbed down the stairs to Platform 4.

The chai stall here was much bigger than the one where Stan worked. I pictured him running up and down the platform serving chai. Sleeping on a bench in the waiting room. Laughing and puffing out his chest like a superhero.

Pushing these thoughts aside, I brought my attention back to the chai stall in front of me. It stood in the middle of the platform and had four counters, one on each side.

There were three men manning it, one old and two young, serving tea and snacks. I perched at the least busy counter. One of the younger guys, wearing a pink shirt, slid a plate of samosas across the counter to a man standing next to me. Steam wafted up as the man broke a samosa in half. He put the two halves in a soft white bun and sprinkled them with red garlic and coconut chutney. My mouth watered and I quickly looked away, swallowing.

"One cutting chai and a small package of Parle-G, please," I said. That was all I could afford.

"Coming right up, miss," said the older man as pink-shirt guy moved to another counter. The old man poured me a small glass of tea and slid it slowly toward me along with the biscuits.

"Thank you," I said.

"Match made in heaven." He smiled.

"Sorry?" I said, dunking a biscuit in the tea.

"Chai and Parle-G, beta." The old man tapped the counter with his wrinkled hand. "It's a match made in heaven. Like Salim and Anarkali. Like flowers and rain. Like the moon and the sea."

I smiled. "It's my favorite."

"And so it should be. Hot spicy chai and crumbly sweet biscuit. When they come together, do you know what they make?"

"Umm . . . a soggy biscuit?"

The old man laughed, and the wrinkles on his face danced a merry dance. "It makes shayari."

"Poetry?" I asked, surprised by the unexpected answer.

"Yes, beta. There's poetry all around us everywhere. Even in chai and Parle-G."

"Arre, Chacha!" Pink-shirt guy turned and glared at the man serving me. "Don't go starting with your poetry first thing in the morning."

"Leave it, Sonu." The third guy slapped pink-shirt guy's shoulder, and they went back to serving customers. The old man sighed.

"Chacha," I said, "what kind of poetry do you like?"

His face lit up like a full moon. "The question should be what kind of poetry do I *not* like? And the answer is of course, none."

I smiled.

"Beta, poetry runs in our blood, it soaks our breath, it colors our dreams." He nodded at the two guys behind him and said quietly to me, "Poetry lives within us, even if, like these two, you don't know or don't care."

My eyes glistened as I thought about how alive poetry was within you, Kay-Kay.

"Take our own on Gulzar saab." Chacha pointed at a framed photo of the famous poet hanging inside the stall.

"Millions of people enjoy his Bollywood songs. They sing and dance and laugh and cry listening to them. All because of Gulzar saab's poetry. They *feel* because of *poetry*."

"My brother writes poetry," I told him.

"Splendid! So, you understand?"

"Yes, but you know, Chacha . . . he's . . . he's . . ."

"Are you all right, beta?" Chacha's walnut-brown eyes filled with concern.

"He's missing. He went missing on a train . . ." I choked up.

"Your brother?"

I nodded.

Chacha didn't say anything. He looked at me his expression a mix of sadness and kindness, for a few moments.

I took your photo out of my backpack and showed it to him. "He went missing on the ERS–Lamora Express on the night of May thirteenth. No one has seen him since."

Chacha squinted at the photo, and his forehead creased. He took the photo and peered at it closely as if scrutinizing a specimen in a lab under a microscope.

"The night of May thirteenth, you say?" He looked at me.

"Yes . . . yes, that's right," I said.

He looked back at the photo. "And he likes poetry, you say?"

"Yes, he loves it. He writes poems. Lots of them!" My words tripped over themselves.

"I think . . ." Chacha nodded. "I think I met him that night."

My heart started beating faster. "You did?"

He nodded, tapping the photo with his finger. "Yes, it was him. I remember because when he saw Gulzar saab's photo, he started talking to me about poetry. Hardly anyone notices the photo, you know, and even if they do, it's rare for them to start up a conversation about it."

I couldn't believe my ears. "What—what did he say?"

"Oh, we talked about Gulzar saab's poetry, and some of Akhtar saab's too, while he drank chai."

"Anything else?"

"Well, we may have made some small talk like people usually do. But what I remember is our chat about poetry. I remember because it's not every day that I meet a young man who loves poetry. I remember he talked about his favorite poet—Akhil Katyal-ji and how much he'd like to meet him. We had the most wonderful discussion. In fact, we got so carried away talking, when the train horn bleated, your brother rushed to pay for his chai and had to scramble to get back on the train, as it had started moving already."

"So . . . Karthik got off the train, drank tea chatting with you, and then got back on the train again . . . That's all?"

"Yes." Chacha nodded.

Thump! went my heart like a bird slamming against a window. I stared into nothingness for a moment. Flies buzzed around the half-eaten biscuit on the plate. My tea began to go cold.

"Beta?" Chacha's voice was gentle. "Here, have another cup of tea."

Wavy strands of steam floated up from the cup as he poured out more chai.

"Sorry there wasn't any more to tell," he said softly. "But . . ."

I looked at him.

"But now you know something that you didn't before. Your brother *was* here. I saw him that night. So whatever happened must have happened after he got back on the train."

I blinked. Chacha was right.

"Thank you," I said.

He smiled. "Drink up your tea before this one, too, gets cold."

"Is there really nothing else you remember from that night?" I picked up the cup.

"No, beta." Chacha shook his head. "Not about your brother, anyway."

I put the cup down on the counter, spilling a few drops of tea as I did so. "What do you mean?"

"There was some hullabaloo that night with the train being held on the platform. It's a long halt at this station anyway, because they have to connect two banker engines to help the trains up the mountain. So that night, when the train was delayed further, people weren't too happy. I think that might've been why your brother woke up and stepped out of the train. Anyway, the stationmaster and the ticket checker argued and argued until they got the problem sorted out. But these things happen every now and then." Chacha shrugged.

My brain buzzed.

What if the hullabaloo didn't end on the platform? What if it boarded the train with the ticket checker? And what if you got caught in it somehow?

I gulped the remaining chai and took out my lists from my backpack. As I scribbled, Chacha peered at me. "Do you think the train delay could have something to do with your brother going missing?" he said.

"It's possible." I folded up the paper and put in my

jeans pocket. "I don't know, but I have to find out."

He nodded. "Go to Singh Madam. She will help you."

"Singh Madam?"

"Yes, she is the duty stationmaster today. She's one of the best and she's very kind." He pointed at Platform 1 and said, "See that office next to the exit? That's where she'll be."

I nodded and took out my nearly empty wallet to pay for the chai and biscuits.

"No, no." He shook his head.

"But—"

He pushed back my hand clutching the wallet.

"Thank you," I whispered.

He waved his hand in the air. "Ah! It's nothing!"

"Not only for the chai and Parle-G, Chacha. For . . . for . . ." I couldn't find the right words.

"I hope you find your brother soon, and remember: poetry lives within us all." Chacha's eyes sparkled. "Now hurry. Go talk to Singh Madam before she gets too busy."

I headed back to the footbridge feeling a lightness in my body. I imagined you and me together at the stall, sipping tea, eating Parle-G biscuits, and listening to Chacha talk about poetry.

Poetry that runs in our blood, soaks our breath, and colors our dreams.

32

STATIONMASTER—ARAVALI JUNCTION

I pushed the double doors beneath the sign. Expecting a small office, I was surprised to find myself standing in a room the size of a badminton court, filled with people sitting at computers. A big electronic whiteboard on the far wall showed train lines crisscrossing each other, with tiny bulbs highlighting each station.

A man with a thick bushy mustache popped his head up from behind a computer screen. "May I help you?" He stared at me.

"I want to speak to Singh Madam, please."

"Singh Madam?" He tapped his pen on the desk. "Why?"

"I had a few questions for her . . . about trains."

"Questions?" His eyebrows arched up. "What questions?"

"About this train that—"

"Arre, Kumar!" came a woman's high-pitched voice from behind another computer screen. "She must be one of those kids from that school. Some sort of transport project or something."

Kumar tutted. "Madam, na! I don't understand why she agrees to all these kinds of useless requests. As if we don't have enough to do around here."

I kept my mouth shut. If their assumption would get me to meet Singh Madam, I wasn't going to correct them.

"Why're you complaining? It's not like Madam is asking you do anything. As if she would!" said the woman.

Kumar huffed, then looked at me, flicking his hand toward a green door at the back of the room. "Over there. Madam is in her office."

The woman chuckled as I walked behind their desks toward the green door.

I knocked on it.

"Come in," said a voice.

A woman with neatly combed hair tied up in a bun was working at her desk. She looked up and her shapely eyebrows squeezed the round red bindi between them. "Yes?" she said.

"Singh Madam?" I stepped inside.

She nodded. "And who are you?"

"My name is Lena."

"And what can I do for you, Lena?" she asked, smiling.

"Please may I ask you some questions?"

"Let me see now." She flicked a glance at her watch. "You'll have to be quick. We're expecting the railway general manager today. So I can only give you ten minutes, OK?" She pointed at the empty chair in front of the desk.

"Thank you." I sat down.

"This is about your school transport project, right? I hope you came prepared with a list of quest—"

"Actually, Madam, I came to ask you about something else."

"Oh, really?" She tilted her head to one side. "You're from New Era School, right?"

I shook my head.

She looked at me, tapping her pen on the desk.

"I have only one question about one train, Madam," I said quietly. "Chacha at the chai stall on Platform 4 said you'd help me. He said that you're very kind and are the best stationmaster this station has ever had."

Her face froze in a hard stare. Any moment now, I thought, she'd ask me to leave. But instead, she laughed a short, warm laugh and said, "Chacha! Did he show you Gulzar saab's photo?"

"Yes." I smiled. "We talked about poetry."

"Chacha sure does love poetry." She smiled back. "OK. Fire away!"

"Why was the ERS–Lamora Express delayed at this station the night of May thirteenth?"

Surprise strolled on her face as she raised one eyebrow and asked, "That's an awfully specific question. May I ask why you want to know?"

"Umm . . . actually, Madam . . ." I wiped my hands on my jeans. "My brother, he—we—"

An urgent knock sounded on the door and she held up a finger at me, as if saying, *Wait a minute.* She looked at door and said, "Come in."

The door banged open and Kumar strode in. "Madam, you'll have to come now. There's a points failure."

She sighed. "Again?"

"Sorry, Madam."

She stood up and looked at me. "I'm sorry, Lena. I have to go. Why don't you come back later?" She was already walking around her desk toward the door.

"Tomorrow. Madam's too busy today." Kumar frowned at me. "Come tomorrow."

"It won't take long. Please, I'll just come back later . . ." My words fizzled in the air as they both hurried out the door. I followed them into the control room, where a few people were gathered around the electronic whiteboard talking loudly.

As Singh Madam's calm, commanding voice silenced everyone, I left.

That day, Kay-Kay, time moved slower than a slug as I waited to speak to Singh Madam. I stationed myself on an empty bench on Platform 1. Morning had turned to noon when a short, stout man dressed in a brown suit stormed into the station, barking orders at everyone around him. I watched as the control room's doors flapped open and closed every few minutes, with stricken-faced people rushing in and out. Chai-wallahs carried trays leaden with enough teacups for an entire village. I hankered for a cup of chai too but then thought better of it, recalling my almost empty wallet.

Remember how when I was little, I would bug Ma and Dad for a cup of tea every time they had one? I simply couldn't understand why I was forced to drink plain old boring milk when the grown-ups loved drinking tea. It was you who gave me my first taste of chai. You poured some of yours into my cup of milk. I took a loud slurpy sip, then smacked my lips and said "Wah!" like the people in the TV ads. As you, Ma, and Dad looked on laughing, I finished drinking the milky tea in seconds. It was also you who taught me how to make chai, showing me how to grate ginger and how long to let the tea boil before adding the milk and how to know by looking at the chai's color if it's fikki or kadak.

You were always teaching me, weren't you? You taught me so many things.

And what did I do? Teased you, bugged you, and got you in trouble.

Like when I insisted on climbing the mango tree and then got stuck. You had to come help me—I still remember how your arms got covered in scratches and grazes. Or when I snuck out to go to the funfair even though Dad had forbidden it. Then when you came to find me, I made you go on all the rides with me one more time and then we got home so late, Dad was mad. You took the fall for it. You forfeited your own trip to the games arcade with your friends that weekend to make up for it, even though you knew Samir would give you hell. Oh, and that time when we were on a vacation in Mumbai and I was obsessed with

Khau Galli and got you to persuade Ma and Dad to let us go and then when we got there, I insisted on trying everything—vada pav, Chinese dosa, masala sandwich, pav bhaji, and of course pani puri. While I took a bite here and there, sampling the dishes and quickly growing tired of them, you were left to finish them and was it any surprise then that you fell ill the next day and had to spend the rest of the trip cooped up in the hotel room?

But you never got mad, Kay-Kay. You never even complained. Even when I'd say sorry (because I do always feel sorry, you know), you'd just smile or laugh it off.

That morning as I sat there outside the control room, my thoughts kept hovering over all those times, filling me up with guilt. When the stout, brown-suited man left with his coterie, the entire station seemed to breathe a sigh of relief, me the loudest. I refocused my thoughts on the present as I made myself wait for another half hour before poking my head through the control room door.

"Back here again?" Kumar tutted from behind his desk. "I told you, na, we're very busy today. Come tomorrow, OK?"

"But I just—"

"Tch . . . tch . . . tch . . . let us eat our lunch in peace, na . . . Go. Go, now." Kumar shooed me away.

I went back to the bench.

I must have nodded off, because when I opened my eyes, Sharabi Baba's bloodshot eyes were staring right into mine. I recoiled, and my head banged on the wall behind me. He leaned toward me and his long, dirty hair flapped on my face. There was a strange expression on his face as if he were looking at me yet not really looking at the same time. As he brought his face closer to mine, a foul smell hit me, and I gripped the bench.

Like a mime artist, his mouth jerked open to flash a set of ugly yellow teeth, then clamped shut into a frown. Open. Shut. Smile. Frown. Then he stared straight at me and said, "What looks like the end of the road is just a bend in the road. And at the bend in the road, something glitters like gold. Reach for it, for that's the key to find what you're looking for."

As my thoughts became tangled in his cryptic words, I heard a man's voice yell, "Oho! Sharabi Baba, stop your nonsense!"

Sharabi Baba jolted erect like a robot and turned around to face Singh Madam and Kumar.

A trembling breath left my mouth.

"Go get Constable Pandu," Singh Madam calmly ordered Kumar.

"No need, Madam." Kumar smirked, crinkling his nose at Sharabi Baba. "I will happily kick this drunk beggar out of the station," he said, rolling up his shirtsleeves.

"Kumar! As I said," Singh Madam said in a firm voice, "go get Constable Pandu and ask him to arrange for Sharabi Baba to be taken to Seva Ashram."

This time Kumar didn't protest and left, mumbling loudly. Sharabi Baba, still in a daze, headed off down the platform toward the waiting room.

Singh Madam sat down next to me. "It's OK, Lena. There's no need to be afraid," she said, putting a hand on mine, which was still clutching the bench.

Slowly, my body relaxed.

"Have you been waiting here all day?" she asked kindly.

I nodded.

"I'm sorry. Why don't you come in the office now?" She stood up.

Picking up my backpack from the bench, I followed her inside the control room.

Singh Madam pulled up two chairs in front of the electronic whiteboard, gesturing for me to sit in one while she sat in the other. She called out to someone to get two cups of tea and the train log and eyed me quietly as we waited.

The chai arrived first. I took a few sips of the hot, sweet tea, letting it settle me.

"ERS–Lamora Express, was it?" she said as someone handed her a black binder.

My shoulders tensed. "Yes," I said. "In the early hours of May fourteenth."

She gulped her tea and put the empty cup on the floor, under her chair. Then she rested the black binder on her lap and flicked through it.

"May . . . the . . . fourteenth . . . Here it is." Her eyes scanned the open page from top to bottom. "Hmm . . . you are right. It was delayed for thirty minutes at the junction. Looks like there was a fault with the points." She shook her head. "It's the bane of my life, I tell you."

"Points?"

"They are the sections of tracks that move, allowing the trains to change lines safely."

My shoulders sagged. "So there was nothing wrong with the train?"

"The train?" Singh Madam's eyebrows squeezed her red bindi as she looked up from the file. "The train was absolutely fine, otherwise it wouldn't have been given the all clear to leave the station."

"And did anything else happen . . . anything strange . . . ?" I asked, trying to ignore the pressure in my throat.

"Are you OK?" Singh Madam frowned in concern.

I swallowed and opened my mouth to tell her about

you, but the control room door banged open. Instinctively, we both turned to look. A man in a khaki uniform entered, clutching a piece of paper in one hand.

"Constable Pandu," Singh Madam called to the man, "please wait a minute while I finish talking to Lena here."

The constable nodded, his eyes flicking to my face. Then he did a double take, looking down at the paper in his hand and back up at me again.

The muscles in my body began to tense.

"It's her!" He pointed at me and scrambled around the desks as I stood up.

"Who?" Singh Madam asked.

"Her!" He showed her the paper in his hand, tapping it furiously.

I backtracked, eyeing the paper. It looked like the missing children posters I'd seen in the police station.

Singh Madam looked at the photo on the paper, and in an instant she was up on her feet. I kept reversing toward the door. "Lena!" she said, and for a moment, I hesitated. But then the constable stepped forward and every muscle in my body screamed, RUN.

I took off, running around the desks toward the door.

"Stop her!" Constable Pandu yelled.

Out of the corner of my eye, I saw Kumar scramble up from behind his desk.

"Lena, wait, don't run," Singh Madam's voice called at me.

"Sorry," I said, swerving around a desk as the constable lunged at me. I sprinted to the door.

"Causing trouble all day! Tch . . . tch . . . tch . . . Where are you running off to now?" Kumar frowned, blocking my way.

I'm not proud of what I did next, Kay-Kay. You would never do something like that. Maybe it was the adrenaline or maybe it was pure panic. But . . . I kicked his shin. He yelped, clutching at it, and jumped up and down on the other foot.

In a flash, I squeezed through the door and ran toward the station exit.

"Stop!" Constable Pandu yelled, giving chase.

I swerved around the waiting passengers, jumped over their luggage strewn on the platform, and zigzagged around the passengers who were on the move.

Constable Pandu's feet thudded after me.

At the station exit, I bulldozed my way through a group of people getting their tickets checked, ignoring their shouts of indignation.

Sprinting out of the station, I huffed across the parking lot outside.

Constable Pandu was still behind me.

I dashed out through big iron gates, and my feet screeched to a halt as I found myself at a busy road with cars and scooters and buses roaring past in both directions. I glanced back and saw the constable's khaki figure barely a few feet away.

Dad would call what I did next *plain stupid*, Ma would say it was *dangerous*, and you'd probably call it *not the best choice*. I suspect it was all of those things. But I wasn't ready to go home then. I certainly wasn't ready to be hauled back by a policeman. All I wanted was a little more time to gather my thoughts, look over my lists, and recalibrate my route.

I braced myself, then leaped into the hurtling traffic.

33

The noise was deafening.

Horns bleeped and blared. Brakes screeched and tires skidded. People called and shouted as I ran through the first line of traffic. Jumping over the white cement blocks dividing the road, I then ran into the traffic going the other way. Somehow, heart in my mouth, I made it to the other side.

Crash! I whipped around and saw an auto-rickshaw slam into a car on the other side of the road. *Was that because of me?*

My feet froze to the ground.

Constable Pandu! I couldn't see him anywhere. *Was he hit?*

My heart froze with dread.

What had I done?

I took a step forward, and the very next moment, a cyclist crashed into me. I fell flat on my face in the road, right into the path of an oncoming car.

Squeezing my eyes shut, I covered my head with my hands.

Screech!

The car scrammed to a halt. As I lay there in the road, still as a rock, the traffic came to a standstill around me.

"Oh, my God! I'm so sorry. Oh, my God! Are you hurt?" said a panicked voice.

I opened my eyes slowly and turned my head to see the hood of a red car, a few inches away from my face.

"It all happened so quickly. I didn't even see you. Are you OK? I'm so sorry," the panicked voice continued.

Pushing myself up, I shakily got to my knees. A circle of faces peered at me. One of them, a woman with long flowing hair, had a halo over her head. I blinked.

"Are you all right?" said the woman with the halo. Her green eyes sparkled.

I nodded, confused. *What . . . ?*

"Thank God!" The woman stepped forward, and her halo disappeared. The evening sun playing a trick on me, I realized. But even without it, her face had something angelic about it. Soft and kind. She was wearing a pale-pink salwar kameez, with a crimson chunni slung across her shoulder.

"Let me help you up," she said, holding out her hand, pink and crimson bangles jangling on her wrists.

I winced as she gripped my sore hand in her soft palm. The small crowd that had gathered around us began to dissipate.

"Are you all right?" she asked again, letting go.

"Yes, thank you," I said as horns beeped and people yelled at us to get out of the way.

"You're bleeding," she said, looking at my arms, ignoring the noises.

"It's nothing, really. Only a few scratches," I said, looking at the rivulets of blood streaming down my arms. Considering what had just happened, it *was* nothing.

As the honking grew louder and the woman yelled, "All right, all right!" at no one in particular, a storm swirled up in my head.

Where was the rickshaw and the car and the constable?

Was he hurt?

I looked at the traffic whizzing past on the other side of the road but did not find an answer there.

Moments later, I felt the woman's hands on my shoulders as she led me to her car and heard her say, "Come, let's get you checked out and then I'll drop you at home."

I sank into the back seat of her car, with worry sinking into me.

34

Her name was Farishtey. Can you believe it, Kay-Kay? When I first saw her, there was a halo over her head and her name actually means angel. Isn't it strange? Dad would call it a simple coincidence or a factor of probability. But you once told me that coincidence is fate's way of righting wrongs. You were right, Kay-Kay.

Farishtey took me to a local hospital. I don't remember how we got there, how long we waited, or much else of what happened. But I remember some things.

The smell of disinfectant and chlorine, like in the swimming pool changing rooms.

An aqua-green plastic curtain. The clinking, clanging sounds of steel rings on a rail.

Red round glasses on a face surrounded with curly, frizzy hair.

The sting of saline solution, the cool stickiness of antiseptic cream, the sharp jab of the tetanus shot.

I don't remember saying anything. But I must've told them my name at some point. Because I remember Farishtey's words, "The doctor said you'll be fine, Lena. The shock will wear off soon."

It *was* shock. But not just because of what happened to me. Because of what had maybe also happened to the police constable who followed me out into the road. Was he OK? How could I find out? Also, I was on a *missing person* poster?

What was I thinking? Ma. Dad. The constable. How many people was I going to hurt?

The next thing I remember is looking into Farishtey's kind green eyes. Moments later, I was sobbing in her arms, telling her everything right there in the middle of the hospital waiting area.

Farishtey handed me the phone. I put it to my ear and heard a faint crackle on the other end. And the sound of shaky breaths.

"Dad?" I whispered into the phone.

He exhaled loudly. "Lena."

A lump appeared in my throat, and I struggled to speak. "I'm so sor—"

"Are you all right? How are you feeling? Did you tell the doctor everything? You've got no other pain or discomfort or anything like that, right?" Dad's words piled on quickly, one on top of the other.

The lump in my throat became a rock. I opened my mouth, but the words refused to come.

"Lena? Are you there? Are you OK?" Dad said.

"I'm OK," I somehow managed to say.

"That's good. That's good. I was so . . ." His voice broke.

I sniffled. "I'm sorry. I really didn't mean to . . ."

"It's . . . It's OK. You're safe. And that's what matters."

"Dad . . . How's Ma?"

"She is OK. She's home now." He paused for a few moments before saying, "She doesn't know. I didn't tell her about you . . . you . . ."

I couldn't bear to listen anymore. I handed the phone back to Farishtey and slumped down on a bench. Putting my head between my knees, I forced myself to breathe slowly. In and out. In and out.

A few minutes later, Farishtey sat down next to me and said, "Your dad is going to come and pick you up from my apartment tomorrow morning, OK?"

I sat up, resting my heavy head on the wall behind me.

"Don't worry. Everything will be fine." She patted my hand.

Slowly, I nodded.

"That's better," she said, standing up. "Let's get going."

"Farishtey didi, thank you." I stood up too. "And, I'm so sorry for . . . for . . . everything."

"Don't be silly. I'm just glad you are OK." She smiled kindly. "If there's anything you need don't hesitate to ask, all right?"

"Actually . . ." I said. "Please will you call the railway station and ask if the constable is all right?"

"Of course." Farishtey nodded.

She looked up the railway station number on her phone. After trying about half a dozen times, she got to speak to someone and was then routed and rerouted through different extensions. She finally got through to the railway police and after briefly explaining the situation, asked after the constable. I held my breath as I watched her listening.

A couple of minutes later, she said, "OK, great. Thank you." She flashed me a smile, then said into the phone. "And please will you inform the stationmaster—"

"Singh Madam," I put in, shaking her arm.

She nodded at me and continued talking into the receiver "Please will you tell Singh Madam that Lena, the girl, is fine and will be going home soon."

After she hung up, Farishtey told me that the constable had turned back the moment he'd seen me running into the traffic. I said a little prayer in my head, feeling the weight lift off my shoulders.

"See? I told you there's no reason to worry, right?" Farishtey patted my back. "Come, let's get going. We'll pick up some dinner on the way."

We headed toward the hospital exit, and she chatted on about whether to get a pizza or Chinese or Punjabi food. Outside, a ripe-mango sun shone in the warm evening sky and a feathery breeze blew through our hair. As we walked back to her car, the relief I'd felt moments ago disappeared like smoke in the mist. Instead, defeat and despair gnawed at my thoughts.

The station constable is fine. But what about you?

Farishtey was still talking as we hit the road. I looked out the window and saw a motorcycle alongside us with an entire family riding on it. A little boy sat in front of a man, and a woman sat behind them, with a little girl on her lap. The girl smiled and waved at me.

"Lena?" Farishtey called. "Pizza's OK, no?"

"Sorry, yes," I said, waving back at the little girl, watching her pigtails dance, feeling a pang in my chest.

"We don't *have* to eat pizza. Just tell me what you want."

The motorcycle sped away with the little girl and the boy and the mom and the dad. The entire family. Together. I wanted to tell Farishtey that I wasn't really hungry. That there was only one thing I wanted.

You. I wanted to find you.

But of course, Kay-Kay, I didn't say any of those things. Instead, I looked at her and said, "Pizza's fine. Thank you."

35

We picked up the pizza on the way to Farishtey's home. She lived in an apartment on the ninth floor of a tall building in a small gated complex close to the railway station. She had been on her way home when I fell in front of her car. Her apartment was small and sparse and sweet, filled with paintings and potted plants.

After I'd showered and changed into a light-blue cotton kameez that Farishtey lent me, she called me out to the living room balcony. I sat down in the empty chair next to her, glad to feel clean again.

"You must be exhausted," she said, handing me a glass of fizzy lemonade and a slice of margherita pizza.

I rested the plate on my lap, feeling no appetite. But my stomach grumbled.

"Eat up," she said.

For a while, neither of us spoke. We nibbled and sipped and gazed out at the carpet of city lights below us.

"I can't even imagine what you must've been . . ." Farishtey shook her head. "What you must be going through!"

I couldn't answer.

"Can I ask you something?" she said.

I nodded.

"What is your brother like?" she asked. Her soft green eyes twinkled.

The question caught me off guard. My nose prickled and my chin began to wobble.

"Sorry, Lena," she said quickly. "How insensitive of me!"

My hand shook as I put my lemonade glass on the little table between us. "No, please," I said. "I *want* to talk about Kay-Kay."

As the stars shimmered and the gibbous moon glimmered, one after another my words appeared. They flew straight out of my heart. They sang and they sailed and they soared. And my heart sang and sailed and soared with them late into the night.

I woke up sweating. For a few moments, I thought I was home, lying in my own bed. Then as I sat up, my eyes adjusting to the dark, the shape of the tall potted plant in the corner appeared, its shadowy tentacles creeping on the wall. I was in Farishtey's apartment, in her living room, on her couch.

My throat felt like sandpaper. Flicking on the lamp next to the couch, I reached for the glass of water on the coffee table. I gulped down the entire glassful. My watch said it was a little after three a.m. I switched off the lamp and tried to go back to sleep. But sleep was too stubborn. She plain refused to return.

I went out to the balcony for a while and stared at the stars and the moon. When I returned to the living room, my eyes landed on my backpack, lying on the floor.

With all that'd happened over the previous few hours, I'd forgotten about the very reason I'd run away from the station. I grabbed the backpack and emptied it. Your poems and my lists tumbled out. So did the newspaper article, which I'd forgotten was there. I laid everything out on Farishtey's coffee table and looked at it all again.

I had not found any evidence, but I did find out that you made it to Aravali Junction. I had also found out that the train was delayed at the station for thirty minutes.

I updated my lists and stared at them for a few moments. A fleeting thought fluttered in and out of my head as if I'd forgotten something. I tried to concentrate by focusing on my breath, the way Nani taught us.

Wham! That's when it hit me.

My fingers shook as I picked up the newspaper article and read it. Once. Twice. Three times, just to make sure.

There it was, printed in black newspaper ink. A clue.

When the train reached Lamora, it was delayed not by thirty but by *fifty-three* minutes.

This could only mean one thing.

The train had made an unscheduled stop.

As I wrote a note for Farishtey, my hand shook, making my handwriting squigglier than usual.

> Dear Farishtey didi,
> I can never thank you enough for everything you did for me. I don't have the words to tell you how grateful I feel. Neither do I have the words to say how sorry I am, for what I'm now going to do.
> I HAVE to go look for Kay-Kay. I've come so far, I can't stop now. And there's this feeling that I just can't ignore. I feel so close. I can't give up.

Not now.

I'm copying one of Kay-Kay's poems for you. I hope you'll understand once you read it.

You truly are an angel.
Lena

PS: I'm also leaving a letter for Dad. Please give it to him.
PPS: I hope you don't mind I took a package of Parle-G biscuits and a water bottle from your kitchen.

This was the poem I copied out:

Two Words

Fear
\ *fiə* \ noun
an unpleasant emotion caused by the threat of danger, pain, or harm
is how the dictionary defines
in black words that sit on a white page
with a simple, authoritative ease

the searing pain that stabs at my heart
the freezing cold that runs in my veins
the howling storm that rages in my head.
I could sit here
let myself drown
in the unpleasantness of it all
or
I could listen
to the little bird singing in my soul.
So I turn back the pages
of the dictionary
from f through e and d to c
to the one thing I need
the strength and ability to do something in the face
of danger, pain or harm
\ *'kər-ij* \ noun
Courage

Writing the note for Dad was even harder. I remembered how his voice cracked while speaking with me on the phone. I remembered Ma's gaunt face looking out through the hospital room window. I really didn't want to cause them any more trouble. But Kay-Kay, that feeling that I had, it was plain impossible for me to ignore.

Dear Dad,

I am so so so sorry for doing this. But please listen.

Kay-Kay's train arrived at Aravali Junction at 2:20 a.m. I found out that he got off the train and drank chai at the tea stall on Platform 4. I also found out that the train got delayed at the station by 30 minutes. But by the time the train reached Lamora, it was delayed by 53 minutes. This means that the train made an unscheduled stop. Something MUST HAVE happened there and I need to find out what.

I don't know what I'll find but I have to do this, Dad.

I need to do this.

I promise I will be careful.

Please let me do this.

It's almost dawn now. If by dusk today I haven't found anything, I'll call you and you can come pick me up. Please give me just one more day and I promise I'll listen to every word you say for the rest of my life.

I love you. And Ma too. Very much.

Lena

I put the letters on the coffee table and changed back into my dirty jeans, T-shirt, and hoodie. The clothes stank, but I didn't care. I folded up Farishtey's light-blue kameez and the bedsheets and stacked them neatly on the couch. After putting my shoes on, I slung my backpack on my shoulders and tiptoed to the front door. With a quick wave in the direction of Farishtey's bedroom, I stepped outside and closed her front door softly behind me.

As I headed toward the stairs, I noticed that the dark was already fading away.

36

The sun heralded a bold new day when I walked through the big iron gates of Aravali Junction. I bought a platform ticket with the last few rupees in my wallet. As I entered the station, the footbridge over the platforms called to me. Chacha's friendly eyes and soft voice called to me. But the clock was ticking. So I headed in the opposite direction, toward the end of Platform 1, where it sloped down toward the tracks, and began to walk.

I walked on as the sky canvas lightened up with hues of pink and orange and yellow. A freight train with boxy mud-brown carriages stood on the tracks at the far side. A yellow temple tower with a saffron flag flapping at the top peered over one of the carriages. Beyond that was a cluster of pink buildings, and beyond that rose a range of mountains, their peaks blending into a wavy plateau.

I walked on with my shoes crunch-crunching on the gravel, as man-made geometric structures gave way to nature's free-flowing designs. Thickets and woods, rocks and mounds appeared alongside the tracks while trains rattled past every now and again.

I kept on walking.

The noon sun shone hot in the sky when the tracks started sloping upward along the incline of the mountain.

My feet ached, and my legs were heavy logs.

My head throbbed, and my eyes watered in the harsh glare of the sun.

My T-shirt was wet with sweat, and my backpack felt like it was full of stones.

I lowered myself onto a big rock under the shade of a neem tree and gulped some water. Then I forced myself to get up again, but my knees shook with the effort, and I fell back onto the rock. I rested my head on my knees.

Did I really think I was going to find anything?

Walking the tracks—what a ludicrous idea!

What was wrong with me?

I wanted to fight those thoughts, but I was so tired, I simply sat there, my head resting on my knees.

A bird chirped from the neem tree, and I looked up.

Chirp-chirp. Don't give up.

I blinked at the green-and-brown sparkling veil above me.

Chirp-chirp. Get up.

A breeze rustled the tree's leaves, and the bird flapped its wings. As it flew away, I slowly stood up.

The tracks separated, disappearing into two tunnels in the mountain. I stepped into the left-hand one, keeping close to the tunnel wall, feeling its cool, coarse stone on my palm. I reached a bend in the tunnel and, within moments, found myself in pitch-darkness; the tunnel smelled musty and damp. My feet slowed down, all of their own accord. In the distance, two red dots appeared. They looked like animal eyes. I blinked and they disappeared.

A shrill whistle sounded, startling me. Then a gust of wind blew in behind me, followed by the roar of an engine. I flattened myself against the cold, damp tunnel wall as a train rattled past, nearly deafening me, its noise amplified by the tunnel. With another whistle, the train was gone, but my ears still felt the reverberations of its roar and my heart still pounded to its rattle. *C'mon, Lena.* I hurried on, toward a faint light that glowed in the distance, and soon sunlight warmed my face again as I found myself on the other side.

When I came to a small clearing by the tracks, deciding I had earned a rest, I stopped and put my backpack on the ground. A carpet of green and brown stretched all the way to meet a blue horizon.

Sitting in the clearing, I ate two Parle-G biscuits and drank my last few sips of water. I needed to carry on but somehow, I couldn't bring myself to leave. I was exhausted, but that wasn't the only reason. There was something about this place, something beautiful and peaceful. Something that made me feel close to you.

I got your poems out, now beginning to look quite worn and tatty, and found this one, which I remembered ending with a celebration of nature. It felt fitting for the place, and I read it aloud.

Wishful Thinking

Wishes usually arrive at my doorstep
in pairs or in threes or in fours,
out of breath, always in a hurry.
Rat-a-tat-tat.

Ding-ding-ding.
I let them in
even though I know
I can't let them stay.
I talk myself into
the same trap again
and I hide them
around the house.

Between yellow library-scented pages,
behind the half-pressed overdue stamp;
under the bed, in a black canvas bag
nudged between the slats, close to the wall;
on top of the wardrobe with the creaky door,
wrapped in a soft, silk handkerchief;
inside the glass jars in the kitchen
between crumbly nankhatai biscuits.

With each passing day
their restless whispers
get louder and louder.
I'm filled with fear
that someone will hear them.
So I brace myself

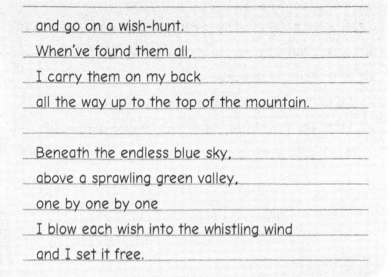

and go on a wish-hunt.

When've found them all,

I carry them on my back

all the way up to the top of the mountain.

Beneath the endless blue sky,

above a sprawling green valley,

one by one by one

I blow each wish into the whistling wind

and I set it free.

A wispy wind whistled from the valley as I came to the end of the poem, almost as if responding to your words. I wondered what you wished for. Then I pretended that there were no rail tracks behind me, that I had come here on a hike with you. I marked an imaginary route up the valley with my finger. I imagined us climbing together like on that day at Bee Falls, teasing and laughing and singing. At the final stretch, we raced up. You let me go ahead so I could claim to have won. And then we stood there, shoulder to shoulder, screaming at the top of lungs for all the valley to hear.

It felt so real. There you were, in your plain white T-shirt, blue jeans torn up at the knees, and your favorite raggedy red sneakers. There you were, grinning your dimpled grin, running your fingers through your hair, pointing at something in the valley.

I blinked and you disappeared.

I was alone with the rail tracks behind me.

You were never there.

37

Another long tunnel later, I arrived at Monkey Hill Cabin, a tiny station nestled in the mountains with a deserted platform that ended almost before it began. I sat on the only bench there, exhausted and spent. A little voice in my head said over and over again, *This is the end of the road. Call Dad.* It had almost convinced me when I heard another voice—a real one—call out to me. "Are you OK?"

A man was approaching. He looked not much older than you, Kay-Kay, and was dressed in white shirt and brown trousers.

"Yes," I whispered.

"Are you lost?" he asked.

I shook my head.

His forehead creased. "Are you waiting for someone?"

A lump appeared in my throat as I nodded. *I am waiting for my brother.*

He didn't look too convinced. "Are you sure you're OK?"

Swallowing the lump, I said, more firmly now, "Yes, thank you."

"OK." He looked at me for a few moments as if trying to make sure I really was all right. Then he nodded and walked off.

I looked around the quiet, deserted platform, feeling a swell of tiredness engulfing me. I called after the young man. "Excuse me?"

He turned around.

"Do you know if there's a phone nearby?" I asked.

"Yes. There's one in my cabin over there." He pointed at a small yellow building behind him.

"Cabin?" My heart skipped a beat. "Are you the signal guard?"

"I am the signal guard, the stationmaster, the helper, and the cleaner." He smiled. "As you can see, this is a very small station and the trains only stop here to check their brakes before going downhill."

I ran after him, not believing my luck. Surely, I thought, this was fate righting a wrong. "Will you please help me with something?" My words came out loud and fast.

"Yes, sure, you can use the phone," he said.

"No, not that," I said quickly. "Please can you check your train log and tell me if the ERS–Lamora Express arrived here on time on May thirteenth . . . I mean . . . May fourteenth, early morning?"

"What?" He seemed taken aback by my question.

"I know it's a strange request. But, please, can you help me? It's really important. Please will you check the train log?"

He looked at me with a strange expression on his face and then said, "No."

I felt as if someone had punched me in the gut. "Please . . ."

"Sorry, I meant I don't need to look at the train log. I know the train was delayed that morning."

My jaw dropped. "What? How can you—?"

"I only started in this post about a month ago. May thirteenth was my first night shift, and it turned out that there was a track circuit failure in the early hours of the morning and all trains in the district were delayed. The ERS–Lamora Express was held too, just before the tunnel that leads up to the station."

His words almost knocked the wind out of me. Another clue!

"What's wrong? Are you OK?" The man's worried

words flew at me, and suddenly I found my voice. "Thank you! Thank you so much," I said, and then I ran.

Ignoring the stationmaster's pleas for me to stop, I dashed down the platform and raced back along the tracks, feeling a new burst of energy in my legs. The long tunnel blipped away and soon I was back in the clearing by the tracks overlooking the valley. I began looking for any signs, any clues, anything that would tell me you'd been here. I knew there was something special about this place. I knew it!

I paced up and down the tracks, looking at the gaps between the slats.

Nothing but bits of newspapers, plastic bags, chocolate wrappers, and biscuit packages.

I scoured the bushes and shrubs around the little clearing.

Nothing but dried leaves and flowers and berries.

I looked under the stones, kicking up dirt and pebbles.

Nothing but insects and dirt and more dirt.

I searched over and over again, not finding anything.

A searing current of rage shocked my body. I picked up stones and dirt and anything my hands could find and threw them.

Then I screamed.

I screamed till my throat hurt.

38

As I looked out over the valley, I found myself thinking something that I never thought I would. I'm sorry, Kay-Kay but at that moment after all that had happened, I was waving you an imaginary goodbye. I shook my head in denial, but I couldn't shake off the thought, feeling the full force of its weight instead.

I needed to head back to Monkey Hill Cabin. I needed to call Dad. Then I heard what sounded like a scream. My head turned toward the sound, down the slope away from the tracks. Several moments passed in silence. It must've been my imagination. I turned to go when I heard it again. This time, it was loud and clear and unmistakable.

It *was* a scream.

Could it be you?

Before I could think about the improbability of this being you after thirteen days, I found myself stepping onto the slope. Because, Kay-Kay, *someone* was down there. And they were in trouble.

I made my way down, careful not to step on any loose stones or grab onto the bushes for support. I gripped the backpack straps on my shoulders as I put one foot forward, resting for a moment, testing my balance before moving the other to join it. I heard another scream, so I picked up my pace, keeping my eyes firmly on the ground, not daring to look down at the valley. I zigzagged my way down in the direction of the screams as the heat of the sun burned my neck and the effort of concentration burned my eyes.

The sudden rattle of a passing train startled me, and I lost my footing. My feet skidded on the dirt and my arms shot out in an attempt to keep me upright. My hand grabbed at a bush and somehow my feet stopped. Breathlessly, I stared at the crumpled leaves in my hand trying to regain my composure. A few shaky breaths later, I moved my gaze to the slope, trying to find signs of the person in trouble.

There was no one there. No one at all.

I looked up at the clearing by the tracks. It already looked so far away. A little voice in my head cackled, laughing at my stupidity.

Why would anyone be out here? Why would anyone be as foolish as me?

As I started to make my way back up, I heard some rustling, shuffling noises behind me. When I turned to look, I saw a strange-looking bird with brown and gray feathers and long stick-like legs take off from the bushes below. As it flew away, I heard its call.

The screams I had heard were birdcalls.

Birdcalls!

I grimaced in frustration. Just then, I caught sight of something glinting close to the bushes from which the bird had emerged.

I peered down.

There was *definitely* something there.

The second hand on my watch tick-tick-ticked in the silence as I stared in the direction of the glinting object. I looked up the slope toward the clearing and the train tracks and then back at my watch. All of a sudden, Sharabi Baba's cryptic words flashed in my head.

End of the road is just a bend of the road.
Reach for what glitters like gold.
Key to what you're looking for.

Whether or not his words had anything to do with

anything, I knew I couldn't leave without finding out what that object was. As I stood there on the slope looking down, I somehow felt as if everything that had happened was meant to happen. It was meant to lead me here.

In front of me was a dirt slope covered in scrub, which got steeper as it went down, eventually plunging into the valley. My eyes darted from bush to bush, shrub to shrub. *Where is it?* I took a few sidesteps and then saw another glint. Just a few more steps.

Foot down. Test. Foot down again.

My pulse raced as—slowly, ever so slowly—I finally made it to the spot.

There it was. A watch glinting in the sun.

My hands shook as I carefully picked it up.

I rubbed the dirt off it and turned it over. I stared at the words engraved on the back:

For Kay-Kay with love

Time slowed and I could almost hear the pieces of fate clicking into place. I kissed the watch again and again as the maddening rush of euphoria blazed through my veins. I wanted to scream and laugh and jump up and down. I was so ecstatic that I'd *actually* found your watch that at first

I didn't pause to think about what that meant. But then wave after wave of realizations came crashing over me.

You got out of the train when it made its unscheduled stop.

You walked to the edge of clearing.

You stood looking out at the valley.

And then . . . and then you . . .

I told myself to stop thinking and put your watch safely in my pocket, then started searching. I scoured the ground where I'd spotted the watch, but there was nothing else there, so I continued downhill.

The slope became steeper and with every step; my legs shook harder and my mouth became drier. I stepped on a loose stone, which shifted under my weight and my ankle twisted. I cried out in pain and lost my balance and found myself skidding fast down the slope. Really fast.

An image flashed in my mind.

Of you slipping and sliding down the valley, bushes brushing in your face and stones bumping your elbows and knees. You screaming. You falling.

I don't know how I did it, Kay-Kay, but somehow I forced myself to banish the image from my mind. And somehow I managed to stop. When I saw how close I was to the final steep drop into the valley, I could hardly believe it.

What if I had fallen down the valley and gotten hurt . . . or worse? Then how would Ma and Dad feel?

Saying a little prayer, I forced myself to calm down and think. There was no way I could look for you by myself. But if I hurried back to Monkey Hill Cabin and called Dad, there might still be enough daylight to organize a search.

I looked up at the clearing. It felt so much farther away than before, and the slope looked so much steeper, but I had to do it. I set my face forward and began to climb. Without looking down or turning around, I forced my way up again. It was hard and slow and agonizing. But I kept going, step by step by painful step.

When I finally made it back to the clearing, I collapsed on the ground and buried my face in the warm crusty soil.

39

The forest is a celebration of greens—bright and brilliant, deep and dark, light and lukewarm.

"Look, El-Kay," you say.

"Where?" I mumble.

"There. There. There." You point. "Everywhere."

"What am I looking at?"

"Hope. Happiness. Home. It's here. Everything is here," you say.

My eyes jump from green to green to you.

But you aren't there.

"Kay-Kay?"

You don't answer.

"Kay-Kay!" I scream but my voice gets lost in the greens.

"Lena," a voice called at me from somewhere far, far away. "I've got you, my dear."

Strong, warm arms wrapped around me.

"You're OK. Everything's going to be OK," the voice whispered in my ears. I breathed in the familiar scent of Old Spice aftershave, and my eyelids fluttered open.

There I was, under the kaleidoscope sky, above a sprawling valley.

There I was, in a clearing by the train tracks, sitting in the dirt.

There I was, engulfed in a hug.

"Dad," I whispered.

"Lena." Tears stormed down Dad's face. His arms hugged me tighter as he whispered, "My Lena."

"I'm sorry," I mumbled into his shoulder.

"It's OK. It's OK. It's OK," he said, rocking me.

"I found Kay-Kay's watch."

He kept rocking me, not hearing my words. I gently shrugged him off. "Dad. Look." I took your watch out of my pocket and showed it to him.

His face went pale and his mouth opened but no words came out.

I stood up and pulled him over to the clearing's edge.

"There." I pointed in the direction of where I'd found your watch. Words flooded out of my mouth as I explained to him what had happened and how I found your watch and what I thought might've happened to you.

Dad listened quietly, his face a carousel of emotions.

"We have to find him," I said. "We need to organize a search."

He stared blankly at the valley.

I shook his arm. "Dad?"

"Yes. Yes. You're right," he said, jolting to action. "You're absolutely right, Lena." He took his phone out of his pocket.

I watched Dad make call after call, sometimes pleading, sometimes yelling, sometimes cajoling whoever it was at the other end of the line. Every now and then I would catch him looking at me.

He looked at me in a way that he'd never looked at me before.

He looked at me the way he looks at you.

I sniffed as a little voice pleaded in my head:

Hold on, Kay-Kay.

For a little while longer.

You hold on, now.

40

"**W**ake up Kay-Kay," I say softly.

But he doesn't.

He lies still on the hospital bed, surrounded by beeping and humming machines. Soft pinkish sunlight streams in through the window, lighting up his face. He looks so peaceful and calm, as if he's just sleeping.

But he isn't just sleeping. He's in a coma. Has been for the ten days since we brought him home. When the search party found him by a stream, deep in the valley, he was barely breathing. It was a miracle, everyone said, that he was alive at all. But it won't truly be one until he opens his eyes and calls my name.

The pale-yellow curtains flutter at the window as a gentle evening breeze wanders in, skimming over the bedside table crammed with bouquets of flowers, fruit baskets, and get-well-soon cards.

"Wake up already!" I say, stifling a sob.

Dad puts a hand on my shoulder and I turn to look at him and Ma.

"Shouldn't he have woken up by now?" I ask them.

Ma looks away and Dad exhales slowly. Silence tiptoes around us on the disinfectant-smelling floor. A moment later, squeaky footsteps and the sounds of people talking in the hospital corridor break the silence.

"Lena, you know what the doctor said." Dad's voice is heavy and tired.

"I know, and that's why I've been sitting here talking to him every day since we found him. But it's been ten days now and he still isn't waking up . . ." My voice cracks.

Dad takes my hand. "You can't lose hope now, Lena. Because of you, we found Karthik. Because of you, he now has a chance. You did that. You brought him back."

His words crush me. Somehow, I manage to say, "But . . . he's not back."

I walk over to the window and look outside. No pinkish sunlight sparkles now. Even the skies have turned. All I can see is a gloomy gray sky shrouding a grim gray city. For as far as my wet eyes can see, there is only gray. Nothing else.

41

The next morning, as we are getting ready to go to the hospital for another day, the doorbell rings. I expect the newspaper boy, but when I open the door, I find Samir and Mrs. Pratap standing at our doorstep.

I've never seen Samir look so sober. He is dressed not in his usual skinny fit T-shirt and designer jeans, but in a plain sky-blue shirt and black pants. His hair is neat and flat, with no trace of his trademark gel. His mom, on the other hand, is dressed gaudily as usual in a neon-orange sari, her face plastered with makeup.

A sudden fury grips me as I look at them and I say sharply, "Why are you here?"

Mrs. Pratap tuts and shakes her head. "Is your father

home?" she says as Samir stands mutely next to her.

"You didn't answer." I grit my teeth. "Why are you here?"

She looks over my shoulder. "Mr. Krishnan?" she calls, seeing Dad behind me. "May we come in?"

"Why?" I ask glaring at Samir. He looks away.

His mum huffs and then says, "Beta, we understand you're angry with Samir. But everyone makes mistakes, na?"

"Mistakes?" I say loudly. "Stealing your best friend's phone is a mistake? Lying about it is a mistake?"

"It's all right, Lena," Dad says quietly.

"It's not all right, Dad," I say. "He stole Kay-Kay's phone—and didn't own up, even when he was missing for days. How is that all right? How can he stand there and pretend he doesn't understand what he did?"

"He feels bad, beta." Mrs. Pratap steps forward.

"Feels *bad*?" I block her way and glower at Samir, who's now staring at his feet. "You feel *bad*, do you? What exactly do you feel *bad* about?"

Dad tries to calm me. "Lena, it's OK—"

"No!" I yell. "What exactly do you feel *bad* about, Samir?"

Mrs. Pratap puts a hand on my shoulder. "Look, my son just wants to apologize—"

"Apologize? Really?" I slap off her hand and stare at Samir's red face.

"I'm . . . I'm s-s-sorry for . . ." Samir stutters.

"For what? For being a weasel and a liar and a horrible, horrible friend?"

"Mr. Krishnan, say something to your daughter, please. There's no need for language like this. Samir just made a mistake." Mrs. Pratap huffs. "This really is uncalled for."

"After everything that has happened, I think Lena's anger is completely called for." Dad's voice is calm and even and strong.

Samir squirms in his shoes. Mrs. Pratap's face contorts with shock. "How can you say that, Mr. Krishnan? This is so insulting!"

"Insulting?" Dad says.

"Yes! Insulting!" Mrs. Pratap huffs. "We are *decent* people, Mr. Krishnan. I know Samir made a mistake. That's why I brought him all the way here to your home, so he could apologize. But instead of listening, your rude daughter is yelling and calling my poor son names, and you . . . you are defending—"

"You know what, Mrs. Pratap?" Dad holds up his palm. "My daughter has more courage, integrity, and decency than your son could ever dream of having. More than I could even . . ."

"Dad . . ." I whisper as he turns to look at me, unblinking behind his spectacles.

Then he looks back at Mrs. Pratap and says, "Let us not drag this any further than it needs. Please say whatever it is that you've come to say. We all know why Samir is here. Principal D'Angelo called to tell me the terms of his probation. I also know that the police didn't want to let him off so lightly. Inspector Rana told me that Samir confessed to starting the fire in the chemistry lab—"

"What? No! That was an accident." Mrs. Pratap goes red. But quickly, she straightens her shoulders and prods her elbow into Samir's stomach. "Tell them, Samir beta. Tell them that it was an accident—"

"Accident or not, the fire caused injuries," Dad says. "Shouldn't your son have told the truth and apologized right after the incident?" Dad shakes his head. "And when Karthik tried to convince him to do the right thing, shouldn't he have listened to his friend instead of fighting with Karthik and stealing his phone to destroy evidence . . ." Dad looks at Samir. "Just think, if Samir hadn't lied to the police, they might've found my son sooner. He might not have suffered . . . He might not be lying in the hospital like . . ."

My throat tightens as image after image flashes in my mind like a nightmare.

Kay-Kay on the ground, broken, barely breathing, but somehow holding on.

Kay-Kay on the stretcher being rushed into the operating room.

Kay-Kay on the hospital bed, hooked to machines, deep in a coma.

I look at Samir again. "If it was me, I would've turned you in without a moment's hesitation. But not Karthik. He must've agonized over his decision. He must've tried everything to convince you, to help you. No wonder he was up at dawn that night on the train. And I bet you didn't even lose one wink of sleep, did you?"

Samir doesn't meet my eyes. He doesn't say anything.

Dad clears his throat. "You are lucky, Samir," he says. "Principal D'Angelo is giving you a chance by not pressing charges. So, please, I urge you, say what you came to say and leave."

Mrs. Pratap prods her son again. "I apologize," he mumbles. Mrs. Pratap opens her mouth, but before she can utter another word, I slam the door shut.

The late-afternoon air smells of anticipation. It is sweet and fresh, and I know the monsoons are on their way. Happy sounds of neighbors laughing and talking drift into our living room.

Ma and I are looking through old photo albums to pick some photos to put on Kay-Kay's hospital bedside table. I flick through an album with a green and gold cover. I look at a photo of Kay-Kay and me from a few years ago. He is pointing at something, his face lit with wonder. I'm looking at him with my mouth slightly open.

"Ma?" I go to sit next to her on the sofa. "Where was this?"

She gazes at the photo, brushing it gently with her long fingers. Kay-Kay looks so much like her. The same sharp nose, high cheekbones, and arched eyebrows. She closes her eyes, and I feel a pang in my chest as I think of Kay-Kay still on the hospital bed.

When will you wake up?

"Jaipur," Ma says. "I remember it as if it was yesterday. We went to the Jantar Mantar, and Karthik got so excited when he saw the ancient observatory. He ran up and down, driving the tour guide crazy with his questions."

A memory knocks at my mind's door and I let it in. I remember a huge stone circle and lots of triangular structures and a large upside-down heart-shaped building with a staircase in the middle. "Can you see the shadow?" I hear Kay-Kay's excited voice. "Do you know this is the world's largest sundial? Isn't it amazing?" I feel his hand gripping mine as he points at the stone structure.

"Yes, it is," I whisper to myself.

I hear Ma sniffle, and it startles me. For a moment, I think she's peered inside my head and seen my memory. But she's looking at a photo in a different album. I see a picture of baby-me lying on a bed as little Kay-Kay, standing on his tippy-toes looks on. Baby-me is smiling, her legs up in the air, pedaling an invisible bicycle, as little Kay-Kay looks at her with a rattle in his hand.

"There's always been something special about you two," Ma says softly.

"Special?" I ask.

She nods. "An invisible, unbreakable bond. Right from the moment you were born. While I was in labor, Karthik stayed with your nani. When we arrived back from the hospital, they were waiting by the building gates. Karthik had insisted on it. 'I won't go home without my baby sister.' That's what he said to your nani. We'd got caught in traffic and they'd waited there for over an hour. Karthik was not even three years old."

My eyes glisten as I listen to Ma continuing wistfully. "You had colic when you were a baby. Sometimes you'd cry for hours. I tried so many things—gripe water, home remedies, but nothing would soothe you. I'd feel so helpless. And then you'd hear your brother's voice and you'd calm down immediately . . ."

Ma's words make my heart ache, and I remember the conversation I overheard when she was in the hospital.

"I'm sorry," I blurt out.

"Sorry?" Ma's eyebrows crisscross. "For what?"

I stare at my hands on top of the photo album in my lap. "I know I'm the reason for your . . . your illness . . ."

Ma inhales sharply and doesn't say anything. I can't bear to look up.

"My . . . my illness . . . ?" Her voice cracks.

I chew at my fingertips.

"My illness is just that. An illness—a mental-health condition. It can happen to anyone, anywhere, anytime. You did not cause it."

My chin wobbles as I force myself to look at her. "But you said to Dad, it was my birth that brought it on. And I thought that . . . maybe . . . that is why you love Kay-Kay more than me."

Tears streak down Ma's cheeks as she takes my hands and grips them tightly in her own.

Why did I even open my mouth? Just when she's starting to feeling better.

"I'm sorry," I whisper.

"No, Lena, I am sorry," she says, looking me in the eye. "I am sorry you had to hear those words. I am sorry I ever said them. I can only imagine how much they must've hurt you. I was so wrapped up in my own pain that I couldn't see or think of anything else. Please forgive me, Lena."

I stare at Ma's glistening face as the warmth of her words seeps through me.

"And I want you to know that I couldn't be happier or prouder to be your mother," she says softly.

"Really?" I say.

"Truer words have never left my mouth." Ma gently touches my cheek. In the next moment, I wrap my arms around her and fill myself up with her Ponds talc scent and her true words.

The night is hot and thick and restless as I look out my bedroom window up at the starless sky. The new school year is starting in a couple of days, and I can't bear the thought of going back when Kay-Kay's still in the hospital. There's a knock at the door, and I turn to see Dad poking his head inside.

"Can I have a word?"

I nod and he comes in.

"Can't sleep?" He sits down on my bed.

"No." I shrug.

"Me neither." He taps on the bed.

I sit down next to him, and neither of us says anything

for several moments. Then Dad says, "Ma told me about your conversation."

I bite my lip.

"Are you OK?"

I nod.

He lets out a loud breath. "I am glad you two spoke."

"Me too," I whisper.

Dad takes his glasses off and rubs his eyes. Then he looks at me and says, "I am sorry too, Lena."

"Sorry? For what?" I ask.

He sits quietly a few moments, then says, "For so many things. I should've listened to you and protected you and stood up for you, but instead I let my misguided thinking make me side with the police and the likes of Mrs. Pratap." Dad's voice trembles as he continues, "Had I listened to you, we would've found Karthik sooner. It's my fault he's lying there helpless—"

"No, Dad, it's not your fault," I cut in. "It's nobody's fault. We still don't know what really happened."

Dad stares at me with eyes soaked in sadness. "I have failed. Failed you both . . ."

"No, don't say that, Dad," I whisper.

"I should've been the kind of father who listens and understands his children," he says. "Instead, I was the kind of father who thought that he alone knew what was right. I didn't realize how much pressure Karthik felt, how invisible you felt because of me. I failed you both."

My heart crumbles as I see tears slip out of his eyes. "Dad, it's OK," I say. "And aren't you the one who's always telling us that dwelling on our past only makes us lose sight of our present and our future?"

My words float in the air, and Dad looks away. I can see how hard he is trying to stay composed.

"I love you." I sniff. "So does Karthik. And we know that you love us."

Dad nods and looks at me. "You, my dear daughter, are extraordinary. Thank you," he says. "For everything. I promise I shall be a better father from now on, to you both."

His words fill me with happiness. But in the very next moment, a persistent nightmarish thought forces its way into my head. And perhaps this is the first time I try to say it out loud. "But what if . . . ?" I can't bring myself to finish the sentence.

Dad takes my hand. "He will wake up."

I nod, latching onto his words as tightly as I can.

"Try to get some sleep." He pats my hand and gets up to leave.

"Good night," I say as he leaves closing the door behind him.

I lie down on my bed, staring at the dark nothingness around me. As the night falls into blackness, the air gets cooler and from somewhere faraway I hear the roar of thunder and see the flash of lightning.

Try as I might, I cannot sleep.

A storm is coming.

42

I shuffle the pale-yellow curtains aside and open the window. Outside, dark, heavy clouds are pulling the sky down, leaking rain. A cool wind saunters in, and I breathe in the wet-earth scent.

"Can you hear that, Kay-Kay?" I say.

Pitter-patter.

Pitter-patter.

Pitter-patter.

I stretch my arm out the window, and raindrops dance on my hand as lightning lights up the leaden sky like Dussehra fireworks.

The sound of the falling rain drowns out the humming and beeping of the machines and the noises from the corridor. I look at Kay-Kay's peaceful face and I want to shake him by the shoulders and scream in his ears.

When will you wake up? When will you come back?

Instead, I sit down in the chair next to his bed and look at my watch. Soon, it'll be time to go home. Then I will have to eat and sleep and wake up and show up to the first day back to school pretending that everything is OK.

I blink and open my backpack to get the wad of poems out, more worn now than ever. I sift through them slowly, one by one by one, tracing my fingers over his beautiful words. Words that let me into his hidden world. Words that he couldn't say out loud. Not to anyone, not even me.

"I'm sorry, Kay-Kay," I whisper. "I'm sorry that I wasn't there for you the way you've always been for me. You listened. You understood. You knew how I felt. And I didn't even know how difficult things were for you. I didn't even . . ."

A lump presses painfully inside my throat. I clamp my mouth shut, close my eyes, and sit quietly, listening to the rain.

Pitter-patter.

Pitter-patter.

Pitter-patter.

"Lena." I feel a hand on my shoulder. "Are you ready to go home?" Dad asks.

No, I'm not ready. I won't ever be ready till Kay-Kay wakes up.

"Please will you give me five more minutes?" I say.

Dad pats my shoulder. "Ma and I will be right outside in the corridor, OK? Come when you're ready."

"Thank you," I whisper as Dad's footsteps pad out of the room.

I put Kay-Kay's poems back in my backpack and fish out my notebook from the front pocket. I drag the chair closer to his bed and lean in.

"I've got something for you," I say, opening my notebook. "It's only a little something I wrote. It's not a poem or anything like that . . ." My voice trails off, but I continue anyway and read out the words on the page:

Five Things About You
1. You are the kind of rare that would make a diamond seem ordinary.
2. A million stars shine in your eyes.
3. Warrior's blood runs in your veins.
4. Kindness lives in your bones.
5. The world is special because you are in it.

I would give anything to walk in your shadows again.

• • • •

Kay-Kay's eyes are still closed. Carefully, I rip the page from the notebook and fold it in a neat rectangle. I put it in the palm of his hand and wrap his fingers gently over it. When I let go, his fingers unfurl back of their own accord.

I look away and choke back a sob.

"Bye, Kay-Kay," I whisper as I stand up. Putting the notebook away, I glance at the closed door behind which Ma and Dad are waiting to take me home. Home without Kay-Kay. The sob threatens to rise again as I pick up my backpack. A gust of wind forces its way through the window, making me shudder.

And then I hear it.

A voice. It's so faint.

A name. It's mine.

It's mine!

I turn around in a flash and rush to Kay-Kay's bedside. His face is still and his eyes are closed. The sob rises up and up.

I must've imagined it.

But then I look at Kay-Kay's hand. I see that his fingers are now curled around the folded rectangle.

"Kay-Kay?" I say in one shaky breath.

His lips part slowly.

I will my heart to slow down and lean in close.

A tiniest, faintest of whisper escapes his parted lips.

"El-Kay . . ."

I freeze. And then it hits me.

"He's awake," I cry. "Kay-Kay's awake. He's finally awake."

THREE
MONTHS
LATER

43

Cool, moist breeze touches my face as I stare out through the bus window. The monsoons have worked their magic on the land, painting it a dozen tints and tones of green with the frenzied strokes of an inspired artist. I stick my head and arm out the window and feel the breeze tickling through my hair and my fingers. I breathe in the wonder of this world.

"Careful, El-Kay." Kay-Kay taps my shoulder. He is sitting next to me on the bus, with an open book resting on his lap.

"Yessir, Mr. Kay-Kay, sir!" I say, settling back in my seat. He grins, shaking his head, and goes back to reading his book.

I twist around and look at Ma and Dad sleeping in the

seats behind us. Dad looks funny with his glasses hanging by the tip of his nose. Ma looks peaceful, resting her head on Dad's shoulder. As I look at their relaxed faces, I can't help but smile.

Here I am, with my family. All of us. Together.

"What are you thinking about?" Kay-Kay asks me, putting his book down again.

"Nothing," I say. "I am just happy."

He nods, smiling.

My nose prickles and I look out the window again, listening to the soothing hum of the bus engine.

"Can I ask you something?" Kay-Kay says.

I turn to look at him. "Of course."

"How come you haven't asked me what happened that night?" His voice is quiet.

I don't trust myself to speak.

Because I'm scared. Because I feel guilty. Because I can't bear to hear about how sad you must've been.

I bite my lip.

"I want to tell you."

I blink.

"Is it OK if I tell you?"

I nod.

"That night on the train, I just couldn't sleep."

"Why?" I ask. "Because of what happened with Samir?"

Kay-Kay nods. "I hadn't been able to stop thinking about him and what he'd done. All through camp."

"The lab fire?"

"Yes." Kay-Kay takes a deep breath. "Just before our finals, I found out that he was involved in it."

I tried to keep my voice measured. So it was true. "How?"

"Actually, it was Samir himself who told me," Kay-Kay added.

"Seriously?" I frown. Admitting to something like this didn't sound like the Samir I knew!

"Let me back up for a bit."

"OK." I nod, my mind awhirl. I try to be patient and let Kay-Kay explain in his own time.

"So. When the lab fire happened, we were all so shocked—I mean the whole school kinda went into panic mode for a few days, you know. Especially my class, as one of our classmates was injured in the incident. The new guy."

"Akash. Right?"

"Yes!" Kay-Kay is surprised. "How did you know?"

"Mrs. Pillai told me about him. She said that his treatment was so extensive that he couldn't take the final exam and now has to miss a school year."

Kay-Kay's face clouds over. "I felt so bad for him. Some

of us visited him at the hospital a few times, but Samir never came. He always seemed to have somewhere else to be or something else to do. I couldn't understand why, but I figured that he felt too uncomfortable or had a phobia of hospitals or something."

"Scared to death, more like!"

"Yes . . . probably," Kay-Kay says thoughtfully. "But he also felt guilty. I only realized this weeks later. One day, just before finals, a classmate put a message on our group chat saying Akash had been told he couldn't take the exams and would have to repeat the year. Everyone started saying how bad they felt, but Samir didn't comment. Later that night, I got a text from him."

"What did it say?"

"It was kinda all over the place. But it was pretty much a confession—about a prank gone wrong that led to the fire. How he didn't mean for anyone to get hurt. How it was an accident . . ."

"A *prank? An accident?*"

"I know, I know! I called him right away and told him he had to come clean."

"And he refused, of course."

Kay-Kay exhales. "Yeah, he refused. Then he started backtracking and saying it wasn't really his fault. That it never would have happened if Akash hadn't joined our class . . . Mrs. Pillai might have told you, they asked me to buddy with him when he was new. So I ended up hanging out with him a bit, showing him around the school and helping him catch up with class work. Sometimes it meant I couldn't hang out with Samir. He didn't take to that too well."

"He was *jealous?*"

"Possibly. But anyway, he didn't like Akash and was quite vocal about it. The day of the fire, he was coming back from karate and saw Akash with some guys doing some extra lab work at lunchtime, so he decided to play a prank on him. *Just to scare him a little bit. Just for fun.*"

"How?" I ask quietly.

Kay-Kay's voice is as quiet as mine. "Samir had gotten some firecrackers from somewhere—I don't even know how he had them on him during school hours. He dared one of his friends to throw a couple through the lab window . . . You know how carried away he gets when he's showing off."

For several moments, neither of us says anything as our thoughts get wrapped up in what happened afterward. Then I break the silence and say, "It must've been so hard hearing all this. Akash was your classmate, your friend . . ."

Kay-Kay inhales sharply. "I actually started feeling guilty about neglecting Samir—maybe if I'd—"

"It wasn't your fault!" *Surely he can't really think that!*

"I know that now. But at the time I felt bad about it. And maybe that's why I didn't push Samir too hard to confess right away. He begged me to give him till after the exams to own up, and I agreed."

"I can understand," I say.

"So I waited for him to confess. But he didn't, and when school finished he started really avoiding me. We didn't speak for weeks. I thought he wouldn't be able to avoid me at camp, and I told myself that if I didn't convince him then, I'd report him myself as soon as we got back."

Oh, Kay-Kay! I already know what's coming next.

Kay-Kay shakes his head. "For the first few days, he walked off whenever I tried to bring up the topic. Then I finally cornered him one day when we were on a hike. Said that if he didn't confess, I'd show his confession text to Principal D'Angelo myself. He got so mad, he kinda just exploded. He even threw in a punch—gave me a bloody nose. I've never seen him so angry. There was no talking to him. Later that day he switched rooms and went back to giving me the silent treatment. I felt like such a fool for having trusted him."

"You *are* a fool," I mumble. "Giving him so many chances to own up. I never would have done that."

"Of course you wouldn't have." Kay-Kay laughs. "You'd much rather knock him out, right?"

"What? You're not talking about what happened at the soccer field?" I punch his arm. "I was angry, OK? And it's not like I hit him or anything. I only gave him a little push. But then he tripped and fell and made such a scene. What a baby!"

Kay-Kay grins. "Do you want to hear the end of this story or not?"

I make a face but let him continue. "That night on the train home from camp, I couldn't sleep. I kept thinking about the next day, how once we reached Lamora, I'd have no choice but to go to Principal D'Angelo. It was hard, you know—it was the right thing to do, but it also felt like I was snitching on my best friend."

"I don't think I'd be able to do that," I admit. "But then I would never have to do it, either. Ayesha's simply the best!"

"She's a great friend," Kay-Kay agrees. "You're very lucky. You know that, right?"

"Yes."

"So that night, I was still awake at dawn when Samir woke up to go to the bathroom and I found myself following him out of the compartment in a last-ditch attempt—"

"Ah! So, Raheem *did* see you."

"Raheem?" Kay-Kay looks puzzled. "He was asleep."

"I know, I know, sorry," I say quickly. "Go on. You were saying you followed Samir, and then?"

"I told him I'd give him one last chance to fess up when we got home, but . . ."

"He didn't listen, of course."

"Not just that: he actually threatened me. Well, maybe *threaten* isn't the right word."

"What did he do?"

Kay-Kay pauses, considering his words. "You remember the scholarship exam?"

"How could I forget! The one and only time that you failed something Dad went around for days acting as if someone had died . . ."

"I know. He wanted so badly for me to do well. That's why I couldn't tell him what really happened."

"What do you mean?"

Kay-Kay looks at me intently, then glances at the seat behind us. Ma and Dad are still fast asleep. Then he straightens his shoulders and says, "You know how I attended special classes every week to prepare for the exam?"

I nod slowly, wondering where this was going.

"Well"—Kay-Kay takes a deep breath—"I didn't."

"What do you mean you didn't? You went to the classes every Wednesday for like months."

"I did go to class every Wednesday, only it wasn't a class to prepare for the exam."

"Then?"

"It was actually a creative writing class. My English teacher recommended it."

"You went to the young writers program?"

Surprise sweeps Kay-Kay's face. "How did you know?"

"Mr. Anjan told me," I say. "He said how he recommended you for it and how difficult it was to get into and how it's the best in our state."

Kay-Kay nods. "When Mr. Anjan first mentioned it, I was sure I wouldn't get a place on the program. So I didn't think much about it. Besides, it would eat up a lot of my time—the class itself and the assignments and all the reading. And, the class overlapped with the scholarship exam prep class. I knew that Dad would never give his permission knowing that."

He wasn't wrong. Dad would not have been happy.

"But then Mr. Anjan told me I'd been accepted and I started thinking how great it would be to actually attend the program. He showed me the anthology from the previous year, and it was so good, and I imagined what it would be like if I could write like that—if my work could be in it next year. I think that's when I decided to go for it. I convinced myself that I could do both, attend the program and pass the scholarship exam. And as long as I did that, it wouldn't be that big of a deal that I was lying to Ma and Dad and using the prep class fees for the program. It was only nine months, I told myself. If I planned well enough and slept a little less and worked harder, I could do it. And that way everyone would be happy . . . but then . . ."

"It was harder than you thought?"

Kay-Kay leans back into his seat. "For the first few weeks, it wasn't so bad. I was able to keep up pretty well. Samir actually helped me."

"Samir? Really?"

"He helped a lot, to be honest." Kay-Kay sighs. "He helped me keep the secret and covered for me. He even managed to get me the study materials from the prep class through one of his friends. That's how I was able to manage, for a while at least. But it became harder and harder. No matter how hard I tried, there was never ever enough time to do everything—the studying and practice tests for the scholarship exam and the assignments and reading for the program, plus my normal school homework. It got too much. I started getting headaches and having trouble concentrating. And that made things worse—it was like a vicious loop . . ."

I nod slowly even as a dark fear haunts my mind.

"I tried to ignore the pressure and keep calm, but as

each day went on, I felt more and more stressed. As the scholarship exam drew closer, I knew there was no way I would pass it. And that made me feel absolutely terrible. I kept thinking about how stupid it was for me to even think that I could pass the exam and keep up my writing. I kept feeling so guilty for lying to Ma and Dad. I kept worrying about how disappointed they'd be when I failed the exam. It was awful . . ."

The dark fear deepens its hold over my thoughts as Kay-Kay continues.

"So I failed the exam. Like I knew I would."

"I'm sorry, Kay-Kay," I whisper.

"Oh. Don't be. It wasn't your fault."

But it was, wasn't it? At least a little bit. If only I'd known how hard things were for you. If only I'd asked you. If only I'd helped you.

As these thoughts flurry around in my head, all I manage to do is nod.

"Anyway, now you can imagine what Samir would've said to me that night on the train when I tried to convince him one last time to come clean."

"He'd tell Dad why you failed the exam?" I ask as a puzzle piece locks in place.

Kay-Kay nods. "He felt betrayed, I guess. After all, he'd covered for me, so he expected me to cover for him. He called me a hypocrite and a liar and a coward and said that if I didn't delete the text, he'd tell Dad how I'd lied for months about the classes and misused his money and betrayed his trust."

"But that's hardly the same thing as playing a prank that leads to people actually getting hurt, is it?"

"No, it isn't the same. But what I did wasn't right, either, El-Kay. Everything he said was true. I was a hypocrite and a liar and a coward. I did misuse the money. I did disappoint Ma and Dad and betray their trust . . . Anyway, after Samir went back to our compartment, I couldn't bear to follow him. The more I thought about everything, the worse I felt . . . I guess I wasn't just worried about betraying my best friend. I guess I was just as worried about talking to Ma and Dad, owning up to what *I* had done . . . I felt like my head would explode . . ."

I fiddle with my watch strap as I try not to imagine just how bad Kay-Kay must've been feeling then. Suddenly, I don't want to hear the rest. But it's too late.

"I opened the train door and sat down, resting my feet on the entry steps," he continues. "The cool wind blew on my face and after a while of feeling the rhythm of the train and the touch of the wind, my thoughts started to settle. I stayed sitting there even as the sky started lightening up. I was still there when the train made the unscheduled stop near the clearing. When the train didn't move for a while, I stepped down to stretch my legs and stood just outside the train carriage for a few moments. Dawn began breaking over the valley, and the edge of the clearing was only a few steps away, so I walked over to it "

My thoughts flash back to the clearing too, and I feel my body tensing up, bracing for what I am to hear next.

"As I stood there in the quiet, looking at the beautiful colors in the sky, at the gentle light skimming off the mountains, I found myself thinking about fresh starts, new beginnings. I realized that I *wanted* Ma and Dad to know about my writing. I realized that there was *so much* more I was looking forward to."

"Then why did you jump?" I blurt out.

"Jump?" Kay-Kay looks at me incredulously. "I didn't jump, El-Kay!"

His words catch my breath as I manage to say, "You didn't?"

"No! As I stood there, I heard someone scream. Or I thought I heard someone scream. And I couldn't think of anything but helping them, so I started climbing down the bank. But then I don't know how, but I lost my footing and before I knew it, I was tumbling down. I don't remember much after that."

"You really didn't jump?"

I needed to know.

Kay-Kay pauses, then says, "No, El-Kay."

"But . . . but . . . you told me how stressed and worried and miserable you were . . . and . . . and your poems—some of them—are so sad . . ."

"I'm sorry, El-Kay. Please don't cry," he says in horror.

"Crying? I'm not crying," I say even as tears roll down my cheeks.

Kay-Kay gives me his handkerchief. "I'm so sorry I made you and Dad and Ma worry so much. I really am sorry."

Even as I sniff and dab my cheeks with the handkerchief, I feel a weight lifting off my shoulders. Suddenly, everything around me seems brighter and more beautiful than before. I look out the bus window.

At the greens of the trees dancing along.

At the blues of the sky swaying above.

At the golds of the sunlight shimmering down.

I want to etch every color, every shade, in my mind. I want to remember this moment forever.

"El-Kay . . ." Kay-Kay says. "Are you OK?"

Yes, I'm OK. I have never been more OK.

That's what I want to say. Instead I simply nod and turn to look at him. "Can I tell you something?"

"Of course."

"The poems you wrote . . . Some of them are a bit too sad and some of them, I'm not even sure they're poems . . . but they're all . . . they're beautiful, Kay-Kay," I say. "Really beautiful."

"You think so?"

"Yes." I nod. "I loved the one about the sea and the one about Carl Sagan and that one about the blank page and—"

"Wow!" Kay-Kay laughs. "I can't believe you remember so many of them."

"Of course. I told you, didn't I? I think they're beautiful."

"Do you remember the one called 'Two Words'?"

"The one about fear and courage, right?"

"Wow!" Kay-Kay says again. He is clearly surprised. "This is a bit freaky, El-Kay."

I grin. "I may not be a genius like you, but I do happen to have an above-average memory. Besides, who taught you to write beautifully like that?"

"Well then, Miss Above-Average Memory, you might be pleased to hear that it was you that inspired me to write that poem."

"What? Seriously?"

"Yes. Seriously." Kay-Kay smiles. "You know how hard I always find it to go against Ma and Dad's wishes. I don't want to disappoint them. But I have come to realize that that feeling weighs on pretty much everything I do. I'm always afraid I'll end up doing something that'll make them ashamed of me. But not you, El-Kay. You've always been fearless. You've always spoken your mind. You always fight for what you want."

"Oh, c'mon, Kay-Kay. What are you even saying?" I can feel the heat rushing to my ears. "Please stop," I say, even though I feel as if I've won an award or a medal.

"It's weird, huh? Talking about stuff like this?" Kay-Kay grins. "But I mean it. When I see you just going for things, it gives me courage too. I'm not saying everything you do is good, or even sensible, for that matter. But you know what? Even though sometimes you do something and then I get in trouble, it's just good fun and totally worth it."

"Like going to Khau Galli in Mumbai?"

"Well, the eating part was fun even if the getting sick part wasn't." Kay-Kay laughs.

"Oops. Sorry." I laugh too.

"So that's what made me write that poem."

"I hope you keep writing them. Write lots and lots of poems and stories and novels and songs and anything you want." I feel giddy and happy just thinking about it. "And one day I'll show your writing to the whole world and then I will read all your books and make all my friends buy them and go around boasting to everyone that you are my big brother."

"OK, OK . . ." Kay-Kay chuckles. "I will."

"Promise?"

"Yes."

"Sacchi-mucchi, God promise?"

"What did you say?" He smiles quizzically at me.

"It's how Stan says you must promise."

"All right, then. Sacchi-mucchi, God promise."

"You're going to love meeting Stan. I can't wait till we get to Kolar. But, Kay-Kay, can you promise me one more thing?"

"What?" he asks.

"From now on, promise me you'll always talk to someone when you feel stressed," I say. "Dad or Ma or even me. And if you can't talk to us, talk to the school counselor, or your friends. Like your new friend, maybe."

"New friend?" Kay-Kay's forehead creases.

"You know the one from your poem?"

He still looks puzzled.

"*Buddy. Ally. Pal. You.*" I recite the poem's ending.

He stares at me, not saying anything for a few moments.

"You *have* to promise to talk to someone about how you feel," I continue, and shake his arm.

"I promise. Sacchi-mucchi, God promise." He smiles. "And by the way, I don't really have a new friend."

"Oh! Then who is the 'you' from your poem?"

"Do you not know?"

Now it's my turn to frown.

The dimpled grin is back on Kay-Kay's face.

"Oh, no! Don't tell me it's Samir? It's not, right?" I am barely able to keep the panic out of my voice.

Kay-Kay looks at me straight-faced for a second, then bursts out laughing. "God! The look on your face. I wish I'd taken a picture." He is laughing so hard, there are actual tears in his eyes.

"Stop it already." I slap him on the shoulder.

When he doesn't, I huff and look out the window. "Samir! Why did I even say his name?"

Kay-Kay stops laughing. "I don't know."

I look back at him.

He breaks into a grin. "Pagal. Fool!"

I roll my eyes. "Enough already!"

"OK . . . OK." He puts his hands up in surrender. "But you're right, you know, Samir's been my closest friend since primary school after all. He isn't that bad, really. I mean, we did hang out together, did stuff together, helped each other—a lot. And even though he ended up doing all these crazy things, I know he only did that because he was desperate and scared."

"Desperate and scared?" I scoff.

"Yes." Kay-Kay nods. "After I came out of the coma, Samir actually came to the hospital a few times. He was really sorry for what he did."

"I doubt that," I mumble.

"It might be a bit hard to believe, but it's true. I know things aren't exactly easy for him at home. You know what his mom is like? And his dad, is quite scary. He's like super strict and has all these rules . . . over the years, I've heard him say terrible things to Samir. I even remember him slapping him a couple of times—and that was when he had a friend over. Sad, really . . ." Kay-Kay's voice tapers off, and a faraway look appears on his face.

I wait for him to go on, but when he doesn't, I find myself staring at my hands, feeling the tiniest bit of sympathy for Samir. I guess this is what people mean when they say things aren't always black and white.

The air around me suddenly feels hot and heavy, and I pull at the sliding window. It squeaks as I open it wider and stick my head out again.

A gush of cool air blows in, and I hear Kay-Kay call me.

"Yeah?" I say, pulling my head back in.

"You *really* don't know?" he asks.

"Know what?" I ask, puzzled.

"Do you *really* not know who the 'you' from my poem is?" His eyes shimmer with mischief.

I blink as a radiant ray of sunshine dazzles us through the bus window and Kay-Kay utters the words that make me soar high, high, higher than the sky.

"It's you, El-Kay! My sister. My best friend."

ACKNOWLEDGMENTS

Living a creative life is a dream so many of us cherish and a luxury that most of us cannot afford. I feel so very fortunate to be able to receive this greatest of gifts and know full well that it would not be possible without God's grace and the support of some amazing people in my life.

Keya and Vira, this book, and all the ones I'll ever write, are for you both. Thank you for being you and for always humoring your Mimi.

I shall forever be grateful to Ben Illis and Rachel Hamilton, my exceptional agent duo, who saw something in my writing and decided to take a chance on me.

Thank you to the entire team at Walker Books, especially to Denise Johnstone-Burt for giving this book such a lovely home and to Susan Van Metre and Emma Lidbury for showing so much love for it and for being the most wonderful editors.

Steve Voake and Dr. Joanna Nadin, I would not have found my voice nor the courage to call myself a writer without your teachings and encouragement. Thank you for everything you do.

To all my Bath Spa MA WYP friends, especially Ash Bond, Rosie Brown, Helen Comerford, Cathy Faulkner, Nat Harrison, Sue Howe, Leigh-Ann Hewer, Carley Lee, Megan Small, and Izzy Smith, it has been my privilege to have had you all as my writing sisters. Here's to all our writing journeys.

I would like to thank everyone at the Commonword Diversity Writing Prize and to the teams of all unpublished writing prizes—your work is vital to the writing community. And a big shout-out and massive thanks to all the teachers, librarians, and booksellers—you light the way for all of us.

To my friends in the Chaivanists, Gshanks, BFFAE-AEDS, Arvon, MBA, and DD groups, thank you for filling my days with so much laughter and liveliness.

Any expression of my gratitude is wholly inadequate for my parents, my in-laws, and my close family members who are the constants of love and support in my life.

Krishna—absolutely. Thank you for hanging in there with me and for always believing in me even when I can't do it myself.

Finally, thank you, dear reader. Thank you for coming to this book. Thank you for staying awhile. May you journey long and deep in worlds real and fictional. And may our paths cross again soon.